THE POETRY AFFAIR

Dashing Rogues and Ruined Librarians
Book 3

Sandra Sookoo

ARE YOU SIGNED UP FOR DRAGONBLADE'S BLOG?

You'll get the latest news and information on exclusive giveaways, exclusive excerpts, coming releases, sales, free books, cover reveals and more.

Check out our complete list of authors, too!

No spam, no junk. That's a promise!

Sign Up Here

www.dragonbladepublishing.com

Dearest Reader;

Thank you for your support of a small press. At Dragonblade Publishing, we strive to bring you the highest quality Historical Romance from some of the best authors in the business. Without your support, there is no 'us', so we sincerely hope you adore these stories and find some new favorite authors along the way.

Happy Reading!

CEO, Dragonblade Publishing

Additional Dragonblade books by Author Sandra Sookoo

Dashing Rogues and Ruined Librarians Series
Of Dukes and Forbidden Words (Book 1)
Scandal Amidst the Stacks (Book 2)
The Poetry Affair (Book 3)

The Boxers of Brook Street Series
With Love in Their Corner (Book 1)
Go Down Swinging for Love (Book 2)
On the Ropes of Scandal (Book 3)

The Hasting Sisters Series
The Devil's Game (Book 1)
A Second Summertime Courtship (Book 2)
An Impossible Match (Book 3)

Willful Winterbournes Series
Romancing Miss Quill (Book 1)
Pursuing Mr. Mattingly (Book 2)
Courting Lady Yeardly (Book 3)
Guarding the Widow Pellingham (Book 4)
Bedeviling Major Kenton (Book 5)
Charming Miss Standish (Book 6)
Teasing Miss Atherby (Novella)

The Storme Brother Series
The Soul of a Storme (Book 1)
The Heart of a Storme (Book 2)
The Look of a Storme (Book 3)
The Sting of a Storme (Book 4)
The Touch of a Storme (Book 5)
The Fury of a Storme (Book 6)

Much Ado About a Storme (Novella)
A Storme's First Noelle (Novella)
A Storme's Christmas Legacy (Novella)

The Lyon's Den Series
The Lyon's Puzzle
The Lyon's Redemption
Dreaming of a Lyon
The Blind Lyon

CHAPTER ONE

April 20, 1817
Middleton House
St. James's Place
Mayfair, London

G OOD GOD, IF *this rout grows any duller, I might consider plucking out my eyes with a spoon.*

Nathaniel Grossbeck, the eleventh Viscount Holdcraft, gazed longingly at the drawing room windows. Was there any possibility of throwing himself out of one before the night ended? The trouble with doing the pretty at social events was that he didn't enjoy them as much as he did as a younger man, and as each year passed, the crop of young women fresh into society seemed ages away from him in maturity and temperament.

Yet he was expected to marry soon for the sake of his title and to perpetuate the line, for it was no secret within the ranks of the folks who studied England's titled families that the men in his connection had a bad habit of dying early. And frankly, he'd already lived longer than any of them in recent history.

Having one's mortality follow one around constantly makes one want to come the crab.

If he were honest with himself, he didn't fancy wedding a young woman with whom he had nothing in common nor was it likely she would have experience in carnal endeavors, and since he was rarely without a different lady on his arm each week, it might prove a bit of an issue. And that was another reason for his ennui. The current crop of ladies was all the same. Copies of each other, with the same fashion sense, the same way of dressing their hair, the way they spoke and interacted with each other. Where were their personalities? Their sense of adventure? The things that made them unique and fascinating?

Perhaps it didn't matter, for he didn't seek out women for those purposes.

Much.

Mostly, he just wanted to have them in his bed, have a good fuck or two, and then set them loose. He wasn't a rake for nothing, and he'd confirmed that assumption probably more than he should have. Because of that, he'd gained something of a reputation, and those that kept him away from the more upstanding ladies of the *beau monde*, he didn't mind. There was no shortage of women in the other classes, and of those, he had his eye on heiresses more often than not, for what man couldn't use an infusion of coin into his coffers? There was always something on an estate that needed modernization or repair, and those things weren't cheap.

"Oh, Lord Holdcraft, I'd hoped to see you tonight."

The sound of a woman's voice near to him yanked him from his thoughts. He glanced to his side with surprise, for a young lady not older than two and twenty smiled at him. Blonde and buxom, she was every bit the sort of bedmate he would choose.

"Do I know you?"

"I should hope so. I've been flirting outrageously with you for two minutes."

Ah, while he'd been engaged in self-reflection. "Then you would be…?"

"Miss Julia Delaney, daughter of Baron Corden. We met a few months ago at a ball."

"Ah." That didn't help him at all. "Did you wish to dance, Miss Delaney? Or perhaps I could procure you a glass of punch?" Truly, he had no idea why she was talking to him, for he didn't remember being formally introduced to her.

"Oh, I'd like to do something much more fun and satisfying. Come with me." With a bold wink, she led him from the drawing room and the crush therein.

"Where are we going?" Not that he minded, for if she was after a quick roll in the proverbial hay, he wouldn't bid her nay. One woman was as good as the next in that regard.

"I thought perhaps a lovely walk would prove a good break from the crush inside."

To be fair, it was a beautiful spring evening, and miraculously it wasn't raining when they quit the house and moved into the rear garden. "To what end? I am neither a horticulturalist nor a stargazer."

"Oh, I think there will be something out here you're interested in." Then, with a quick glance over her shoulder, Miss Delaney opened the gate at the back of the garden and slipped into the square beyond.

He uttered a huff, for this was largely a waste of time. "Enough of this foolishness. Let us return. We can share champagne and kisses in the butler's pantry." It was one of his favorite places to hide with women for a bit of slap and tickle.

"Why are you grumbling before you even know what I have in mind?" Under the cover of the darkness around them and shielded from prying eyes by a few shrubberies on that side of the garden wall, the bold young woman rested her gloved palms on his chest, lifted onto her toes, and then pressed her lips to his.

What was this? *He* was being propositioned? That was a twist.

And he wouldn't be the rake that he was if he didn't kiss her back. The young woman was no slouch when it came to teasing a man with kisses, so it didn't take long for hot interest to rush through his veins to pool in his shaft.

"Tell me and ruin the surprise," he said between kisses. "Are you trying to get up to scandal, then?"

"Yes, and I'd like to do that by getting something else *up* as well," she replied as she dropped to her knees before him. Before he knew what she was about, Miss Delaney had the buttons of his front falls undone and the placket down. When his rapidly engorging shaft sprang out, she gasped and stared at it with hunger glittering in her eyes. "I'd heard you were well hung, but the rumors didn't say just how much."

Amused but curious as to how she'd do this, Nathaniel remained as still as he could. If she wished to explore, he would let her, for he'd nothing else to do this evening. "Why are you doing this?"

"Why not? I wanted to see your equipage, and find out for myself if you were as good as the gossips say." She traced a fingertip along the side of his member.

Dear gods!

The light touch paired with her tart mouth and the texture from her gloves had arousal streaking through his body. "Proceed at will." For a few seconds, he watched her in the dark and shadows. The moonlight flirted with clouds, sending silvery wisps of light over her face and her blonde coif.

"This is going to be quite delicious, I think." She wrapped her hand about his hardened length, but it was her words that made him more randy than he'd been in a while.

"Do you do this to every man you meet?" Not that he cared or had latitude to judge, for he had quite an impressive record himself.

On a first stroke, she said, "Only the interesting ones."

Obviously. "And you're a social climber." It wasn't a secret, he'd wager.

"Something like that." Then she held him more firmly and drew her curled fingers up and down his shaft.

Bloody hell. He sucked in a sharp breath, for her strokes and caresses had awareness shivering along his spine. "Let me show you how I like it." So she wouldn't think he tried to take control, he settled his hand over hers, showed her how to hold his length to maximum advantage. "Build up the heat. Some men enjoy that, but mine doesn't respond well to rough handling."

At first. There was a time and a place for that, but he rather doubted his relationship with Miss Delaney would last past this act.

After a few minutes of experimentation, a faint smile curved her lips. "I'm quite certain I can get you off, my lord." Soon she was stroking his flesh as if she'd been doing it all her life. Up and down her fingers went, then she had this little quirk that she did at the root, where she twisted her wrist and flexed her fingers, that had heated reaction streaking through his member and into his stones.

With every pass, he hardened further. Need tingled in his balls, but just when he suggested she stop, the damned woman cupped those stones in her other hand, squeezed them with a firm insistence that had his eyes ready to cross.

"I can only imagine how you pleasure women with this prick," she breathed as she glanced up at him with shining eyes in the shadows. "Perhaps I'll find out some day." Not once did she pause in her stroking.

"Mmm." He didn't comment further because they wouldn't meet again. If she wanted to suck him off, of course he'd let her, but she wasn't quite his type for bedding.

"Let's see what else you can do." One of her blonde eyebrows rose in challenge, then with a husky chuckle, she leaned forward and closed her pink lips around the head of his shaft.

Shit!

Nathaniel's whole body jerked as if it had come awake from a shock. She giggled, and the vibrations buzzed around his length, enhancing the exquisite torture she'd already given him. While still holding his stones in her hand, the woman moved closer to him and slowly, so damn slowly he thought he might die, she took his member into her mouth as far as he could go until his tip hit the back of her throat.

To her credit, she didn't gag like most women would. Then, she swallowed, and the contracting muscles gently squeezed his shaft. He nearly shot his wad right there, but he bore down on the urge and gritted his teeth.

"Damnation…"

She drew off his shaft with a slight pop. "God, your member is amazing. A real tasty mouthful." At least she released his stones, and he knew a moment's relief, but it was short-lived, for she slipped that hand around the back of his thigh and took him once more into the warm cavern of her mouth.

In seconds, he was lost in the wonder that was this stranger as she proceeded to suck him off.

Far too quickly, she found a rhythm she'd apparently perfected long before he'd come along. As he remained helpless in her hold, she worked him over with both her hand and her mouth. How she swirled her tongue beneath the head of his shaft, how she tickled his length with said tongue and teeth? Good God, what had she been doing between finishing school and coming out in the *ton*? Well, he had a fair idea, since she didn't deny being a social climber. No doubt soon, she'd snag some unwitting man with a title who hadn't a brain in his head.

Or wouldn't after she was done with them.

With a groan, he buried his hands in her hair, tangled his gloved fingers in those tresses and because he needed some relief, Nathaniel thrust into her mouth.

Miss Delaney didn't bat an eyelash, but there was anticipation and hunger in her eyes. She delved her fingers tighter into the flesh of his thigh. The faster and deeper he thrust, the more frantic and harder she worked him over, and the sight of her blonde head bobbing on his shaft was enough to hurtle him over the point of no return.

This was exactly what he needed tonight. No commitment, but all the pleasure.

Warning tingled through his stones as his muscles bunched and stiffened. His member pulsed, and seconds before he uttered a groan of pure release as he lost control. The release that held him captive was intense, but still she stroked him off. Seconds later, he held her head steady, and as his shaft pulsed, the tendons in her neck worked as she swallowed every jet of his ejaculate.

"Well, damn." His limbs were the strength of cooked porridge. He released his hold on her head. Did she think to say that he'd compromised her and thereby force an engagement? Well, that wasn't going to happen. She might be carnally talented, but he was skilled in avoiding desperate young misses as well as their matchmaking mamas.

And he certainly wasn't looking to marry any time soon, no matter the woman.

When she was finished swallowing, she even licked the remainder from the tip of his member before demurely wiping her mouth with a lace edged handkerchief she must have procured from a pocket in her skirting.

"Did you enjoy that, Lord Holdcraft?"

"I did." As he stuffed himself back into his evening breeches and did up the buttons of his front falls, she stood and shook the wrinkles from her skirts. Shit, he should have taken advantage of her breasts while he'd had the chance, but everything had happened far too quickly. "Thank you for that interlude. You are quite talented in that regard."

"I've had much opportunity to practice." She nodded and let the fingers of one hand drift along the edge of her low bodice, no doubt to encourage his gaze to follow, further tempting him. "Now that we've been introduced to each other, will you call on me this week? I'd rather like to spend time in your company."

Of course she would. Cheeky woman. At least she didn't dance about the issue. For that, he gave her a modicum of respect. "Unfortunately, this is our one and only meeting, Miss… Damn, I seem to have forgotten your name." Not that he cared. She just didn't matter, and he wouldn't see her again.

"Gah!" The young woman stamped a foot. "Miss Delaney. I sucked you off and you can't manage to remember my bleeding surname?"

Ah, good to see that she had upper-class manners. Sarcasm swung through his thoughts as he shrugged. "I don't usually have a drought of women who wish to provide me with pleasure, so therefore, I owe you nothing."

She pouted. "You didn't decline."

"I didn't need to, and you didn't ask permission; you just did it. That doesn't mean an agreement was struck between us just because you crave every dick in London, apparently."

"Argh!" Miss Delaney narrowed her eyes. "You might have a fine form, but you truly are the cad the rumors say you are. I never want to see you again."

He snorted. "Easily done, since I'll instantly forget you the moment you leave my company." This was just how things were. If she didn't soon bring a man up to scratch, she'd have a lovely, bright future as someone's mistress.

"Bounder." With a huff, the young lady strode off, her hips swishing. The gate in the garden wall slammed as it marked her passage.

"I never claimed I wasn't that and so much more." Nathaniel followed at a much slower pace, and after that spectacular release, he was in a rather better mood than he'd been when he'd arrived at the rout.

Fancy that, but then, this was where he was most comfortable.

Inside the house, he didn't wish to return to the drawing room, not because Miss Delaney might be there, but because he'd long ago grown bored of the various societal events this spring. Easter had occurred earlier in the month, so the next thing to look forward to was May Day. Not that he cared. It was merely another day.

Instead, he popped into the library with the hopes of browsing his host's collection of poetry, if any. He might be passionate about pursuing beautiful women—or alternately letting them pursue him—but his love for well-written lines competed with that for his favorite thing.

Before he could peruse the shelves, he spied his best friend sitting in one of the leather wingback chairs, an ankle resting on a knee, with an open book propped on his lap.

"I haven't seen you in an age."

William Sammerson would soon be the new Earl of North-field, for his father was on his deathbed and had been for the past couple of months. They were both the same age of forty and had grown up in each other's pockets, for their country estates in Surrey shared a border.

"Nathaniel!" The man was surprised to see him. "My God, good to see you, old chap."

He grinned. "What brings you to London? I'd no idea you were back, thought you'd be in Surrey until after May Day festivities." There was always a big festival on the soon-to-be earl's property each year to usher in summer, and some years, a travelers' fair set up their encampment at the edge of the acreage.

William shrugged. Sadness was reflected in his expression. "Papa has taken a turn for the worse. His doctor is confident that there will not be a rally this time."

Damn. What wretched news. "His heart will finally fail?"

"Seems like." He set aside the book. "Mama is already mourn-ing, as you can imagine, but since this was coming for some time, it's been a bit easier on all of us. There is a certain comfort in the knowing. Not that it makes the situation less sad."

"I'm sorry all the same." Nathaniel sat in a matching chair. "Is the rest of the family traveling to Town, then?" He hadn't visited with William's siblings for many years.

"Yes. Meredith is set to arrive tomorrow with her husband and brood. Diana should be in London in the next few days."

Just hearing her name sent an odd shiver down his spine. Despite it being years since he'd seen her of had even heard of her, his mind and body couldn't quell that reaction. "It will be good for you to have your sisters with you. I know your mother will be thrilled."

Since their father's estates in Surrey were neighbors, the children had grown up together and, in the summers, they had the run of the land. Until the girls had to take lessons on proper deportment, and he and William were more interested in going to the village to tease tavern girls.

"Indeed." His friend nodded. "Diana mentioned in a recent letter that she's looking forward to being back in society. She couldn't wait to be out of mourning."

What the devil? She would return to Town? Muscles in his gut tightened. Would he have the opportunity to see her? God, what sort of nodcock was he? They didn't move in the same circles. Somewhere in the back recesses of his mind, Nathaniel remembered reading about Diana's husband dying. "Did she despise her husband that much?" He didn't really know much about that sister's romance. There had been a time when William had hinted that he should court the younger sister. Meredith was five years their junior, while Diana was five years their senior.

"I'm truly not certain. She refused to talk about her union. All I know is it was a long marriage, and she's been a new woman since he died." William cleared his throat. "And no, I am not going to ask. It's not my business, and the past should remain there."

"Interesting, but that is a good rule of thumb." In any event, he hadn't seen Diana in perhaps ten years. Part of him wondered what she looked like, wondered if time had been kind to her, but then, he supposed it didn't matter. Diana had been a clever, lively young girl, and he hoped she would have married someone worthy of her.

"In any event, what of you? You seem relaxed tonight." William grinned. "And I know it's not due to your great love of society functions." Sarcasm went through his worlds.

Nathaniel snorted a laugh. "I might have already been brought to release."

"God, you're a cad. You need to settle down. Forge a future you can be proud of."

"Marriage isn't for me."

William shrugged. "You have a duty to your title."

"Perhaps, but that doesn't mean I should rush out and marry

merely to procreate." How dull would that be?

His friend leveled a fond but stern look upon him. "You're getting on in years."

"As are you, William."

"Then we should prowl together. The spring Season has barely started. There is still time to find the women of our dreams, or at the very least, our responsibilities."

He couldn't help but grin. "There is that." Somehow, he'd always known he'd probably wed an heiress in her come-out year, but he would keep a mistress on the side once he'd gotten his wife pregnant. Merely for mature conversation. "How depressing."

"Agreed." After William set aside his book, he gained his feet. "Shall we seek out some of our host's fine spirits and drown our sorrows?"

"Absolutely, and let us leave this conversation for another time." As they left the library, he asked, "Tell me about the new horse you found at Tattersalls…"

CHAPTER TWO

April 22, 1817
Atterbury House
Grosvenor Square
Mayfair, London

LADY DIANA WOODBINE, or the Dowager Viscountess Atterbury, as she would soon be called once her son married—came into the townhouse with a bit of trepidation fluttering in her belly.

The last time she'd been here was two years ago. That was when she'd received word that her husband was dead, shot by accident during a spring hunt put on to bag pheasants and partridges. She remembered sitting in the drawing room with her daughter, reading the letter her son had sent from their country estate in Surrey detailing the accident. He'd asked if she wanted his body brought to London or should they bury him at Atterbury Hall?

Heavens, that had been a difficult time. While her daughter had broken down because her father had died, and she'd loved him, Diana had quite opposite feelings regarding his demise.

There had been an affection between her and Atterbury, obviously, since they'd had two children together, but those feelings had never gone deep enough to mature into love. They'd married because it was a smart match, and he'd needed to do his duty by his title. She wanted the stability of a husband and to have children, for with offspring, she would have people in her life who would love her unconditionally.

Of course, Diana had been thrilled with her son and daughter. They were the joy of her life and well-behaved little souls with good hearts. With her husband? No, she was not thrilled or even proud of him. He never made it a secret that he preferred the company of his mistress, that she was much better in bed than Diana could ever be, that her interests more aligned with his. Perhaps that was because her husband had been almost twenty years older than she, and in many ways, she could understand the sentiment, but having it thrown in her face day in and day out grew jarring after a while.

Eventually they'd drifted apart, and when he finally died, ending their twenty-two-year union, it had come as a relief with a bit of freedom. Did she mourn for him? Yes and no. There had been a few twinges of sadness; they'd been married a long time, and even though there hadn't been love between them—emotionally or physically—for a good portion of that time, he was still her children's father. He'd been the man she'd allowed into her bed. In fact, he had been the only man who had touched her in a carnal way, such as it had been. And along with that, she'd mourned for a life she thought she might have when she'd come to him at the marriage altar as a starry-eyed young woman of three and twenty. Throughout the course of the union, the enchantment and romance she'd always dreamed of having had vanished.

In its place had come responsibility, reality, and motherhood.

Now, she was essentially free. She had the opportunity to choose a man *she* wanted this time around, someone who would bring excitement, life, and if luck was with her, drugging passion into her existence and make up for the years she'd wasted on Atterbury.

The best years of my life, I suppose.

As Diana made her way into the entry hall of the townhouse, she sighed. "It's been an age since I've been here, and I'm not certain I wish for all the memories this visit will surely bring." She'd come to London with a second cousin from her mother's side of the family, Miss Tabetha Potter. Many times, she'd acted like a companion of sorts since Diana had been in mourning, but she was truly one of her best friends, and they were around the same age, had grown up together. There had been many visits between them during the course of Diana's marriage, and long times were spent at each other's homes for visits. It was good to have someone familiar with her now. "I almost dread it."

"Understandable, but it's quite necessary. It will help you heal and find closure, I think."

"Perhaps this is true." For most of what she had left from her husband were unsavory and disappointing memories. "Thankfully, the children will arrive soon as well."

As she gave her spencer, bonnet, and gloves to the butler, who'd welcomed her back with enthusiasm, she heaved another sigh.

It was time to live again, perhaps time to love again, or at the very least, pursue a life she'd always wanted but suspected she'd been cheated from with him. Out of all the times her husband had bedded her, she'd only reached release a handful of those. More often than not, if she wanted that electrifying feeling throughout her body, she had to bring herself to that state with her own fingers.

It wasn't the same, and these days, even that had paled, which necessitated the need to be back in Town. Now that she was officially out of mourning—of course two years was much longer than what was required by society—and her son had successfully taken the title at the age of twenty, she wanted to investigate interests of her own. She hoped Percy would do the viscounty more justice than her husband had.

"They will be happy to see you," Tabetha said as she followed Diana along the corridor toward the main staircase.

"That is the hope." Her daughter was seventeen and in her first year at finishing school in Brighton. All reports said she was bright, intelligent, and charming. These were attributes that would propel her through society when she had her come out in two years.

Yet for the first time in Diana's life, she was alone with nothing but time on her hands. She could do what she wanted and didn't need to consider anyone else's feelings. The overwhelming freedom in that knowledge rocked her to her core.

It was glorious.

"The first thing I need to do after being settled is call on Mama. She's trying to be strong for Papa, and for us all, but it must be a difficult time for her." Of course, there was another reason for this visit to Town, and it didn't have anything to do with wishing to take back her life or have a second chance at it of sorts. Her father was dying, and according to her brother, it could be a matter of days or even weeks. Perhaps he was only waiting until his family could come together for one last goodbye.

"Regardless of the timing, it is good to have you back in London. I've missed having my best friend about. Shopping and taking tea is sometimes stale without you." Nothing but honesty lingered in Tabetha's tone.

"I appreciate that, my dear. And I've missed you too." Diana shoved the thoughts of sadness to the back of her mind. "It is lovely to be back, isn't it? I'm anxious to make my way into society."

Though when her father died, she'd once more be in mourning, for a much shorter time of course, which would further delay the life she so desperately wanted to build for herself.

Perhaps it wouldn't matter.

A grin curved Tabetha's lips and gave life to her round, pale face. "How long will you reside here before your son joins you from Surrey?"

"At least a couple of weeks. Unless Papa dies sooner, of course, then my stay might be longer than that." After gaining the second level, she made her way to the drawing room. Since she'd written to the housekeeper ahead of time, the house had been readied and the rooms aired. As they spoke, the beds were being dressed. It was lovely having a sufficient staff.

Tabetha tilted her head, a habit she had that was quite endearing. "What will you do in the interim?"

"Visit my father, spend time with my mother and brother." She shrugged as she settled into her favorite chair. "I also wish to attend as many society functions as I can. It will help ease me back into being familiar with the movers and shakers within the *ton*. I've already received a few invitations, and I know you have some as well. Between the two of us, we should have a wide range of places to go with hopefully many interesting men to meet."

At least she was honest.

Tabetha nodded. "So, it's true. You're looking to marry again?" She perched on the edge of a low sofa, and in her fawn-colored dress, she resembled a comfortable, chubby woodland creature. But then, her friend was always adorable in whatever color she favored that day.

Was she? Diana nodded, for she didn't need to think upon it. "I am. There are many things I miss about having a husband, and perhaps this time, I'll find one with skill between the sheets, decent enough coffers to provide a future, and the courage to actually love me as I should be loved." That wasn't too much to ask, was it?

"Ambitious list." But Tabetha snorted. "Incidentally, you don't need to marry in order to have a wild carnal life. Just have an affair with the man of your choice."

Diana smiled at her cousin. "While that is true, I want the husband as well."

There was just something comforting and safe about having a man's arms around her, and the fact there was someone waiting at the end of the day to discuss a wide variety of topics as the hush of night fell that made things worthwhile.

Not that she'd had that in a very long time.

"You can have that as someone's mistress," her friend was

quick to add. "That way you needn't be stuck with the man."

"Also true, but I can't see myself as a mistress, constantly waiting for a man to come visit me whenever the whim strikes." She shook her head. "I would like to see if a second marriage will feel different than the first. Surely it would."

I refuse to let a man ignore me this time around.

"Well, I hope you're able to find what you what here in London. I haven't been able to sort through the lists of eligible men so I don't know the bounders from the saints, what with everything else, but I'm glad to have you back. We haven't seen each other in an age. Town just isn't the same without you."

"I agree, and hopefully you and I can have many conversations and outings together this spring." Diana smiled. "How is your husband?" For the past year, her friend's husband had been battling a disease of the lungs that his physician and apothecaries couldn't help treat.

Worry creased the other woman's face. "His illness still lingers but we're hopeful he can rise above it. The dampness of the winter and early spring was rough on him." A trace of tears welled in her eyes. "The promise of sunshine for the rest of the season keeps us in good spirits, though. If he's feeling strong enough, perhaps I'll bring him over here for a visit."

"That will be such a lovely time. I hope he does continue to grow stronger." When a footman brought in a tea tray, Diana smiled her thanks. "There is far too much death in life. The moments left over to us around such things are quite precious. We need to fill them with things, people, and experiences that bring us joy."

"I think so too." Tabetha took it upon herself to pour out the tea. When she gave one cup to Diana, she said, "It is quite true when joy and pleasure temper the worry and sadness. Everything is a part of our life, and we should encourage ourselves to feel all of it."

"That is a very agreeable statement, Tabby." Diana put a small lump of sugar into the amber depths of her tea then she stirred the liquid until the sugar dissolved. "Those emotions remind us that we are alive."

Even through the times in her life when she hadn't wished to be. There were long stretches after she'd birthed both of her children when she thought the darkness might creep too close and swallow her whole. It had taken strong fortitude to pull out of those patches, and with no support from her husband, she felt it was a Herculean task both times. Thank goodness for her parents and her siblings. Otherwise, she didn't know what would have become of her.

Of course, everything had eventually leveled out, and her mind had been her own once again, and for a long time it had remained that way, until about five years ago. That was when her body had undergone another shift of sorts. It had been a transition where the darkness had returned but with it had come a slowing down, or else it had felt that way to her, and in that string of years, she'd realized that she would never again bear a child.

Had her usefulness as a woman come to an end? In a society who judged one by the size of their families and the ability to have sons, had she outlived her purpose? She hoped not. As horrid as it sounded—which was why she'd never voiced this thought aloud—she was revitalized now that her husband was no longer alive, and she meant to enjoy every moment of her newfound freedom.

Without consequences.

In silence, she and Tabetha indulged in the tea service before her friend stirred.

"By the by, are you still a patron of the arts?"

"I am. It's something I find quite comforting and at times, quite satisfying." She took a sip of tea. "Why?"

"Well, one of my husband's friends is searching for a first-edition compendium of Keats's poetry, especially if it includes "The Eve of St. Agnes." I have no idea if such a thing exists, but if it does, this man wishes to add it to his collection." Tabetha added another seed cake to her plate. "If you know of someone who has one, please let me know so I can broker the transaction."

"That sounds quite interesting. Now *I* wonder if it does exist." Poetry had always seemed so romantic to her, but since her husband had held little to no interest in such things, she hadn't read it as much as she would have liked. The young womanly dreams she'd had at one time of her spouse reading bits of romantic poetry and prose to her had long ago died beneath the man her husband had been, but over the past couple of years, she'd started to collect volumes that struck a chord with her soul. "I will ask around to my social circle. Otherwise, I have a contact at one of the local lending libraries, so I could inquire there."

"Thank you. I know he would appreciate it."

She nodded. "Who is your husband's friend? Perhaps I know of him, so if I run into him during events, I could talk with him about that."

"It's Viscount Holdcraft. He's called on my husband a few times during his illness, so that has been lovely. They usually end the visit by playing chess."

"Oh." *Nathanial Grossbeck.* Reaction immediately slammed through Diana's chest, for she hadn't heard that title for a very long time indeed. "Of course I know of him. He's my brother's best friend."

She hadn't been in the viscount's company in many years. Possibly since before she was married, but the two of them had been friends since they were young boys. From what she'd heard of him throughout the years, he'd successfully managed to avoid marriage, but on the other side of the coin, he'd become quite a rake within society.

"I thought he might be familiar." Tabetha nodded. She nibbled at the seed cake. "I've heard through the gossip mill that he has been thinking about marrying for the sake of his title, but he's fighting it all the way."

"Some men don't like to entertain the idea of marriage." From what she could remember, he'd been a wildly handsome and charming young man with hair the color of glowing embers, and he was always quite popular with the ladies. "I hope he decides to marry from the proper reasons, for a union without love is a prison sentence for both parties."

"Not to mention that a man like that will be wasted on a society miss who is just out in society." Tabetha slid a mischievous glance at her. "Perhaps a man like him is someone you should pursue or at the very least try to attract. Gossip has it that he's quite skilled in the bedroom arts."

Heat went through Diana's cheeks. "Don't talk nonsense, Tabby. He's my brother's best friend. We all grew up together in Surrey. Our families are far too good of friends for any sort of romance to bloom."

Would it even be possible?

"Who said anything about trying to procure a romance from the man?" her friend said with a robust chuckle. After she drained her teacup, she landed her laughing gaze on Diana. "Didn't you say yourself that you wanted something different from what you had with your husband?"

"I did, but I could never..." She shook her head. "He's younger than me, besides," she said in a scandalized whisper.

"What does that matter when the clothes come off?" Tabetha's laughter echoed in the drawing room. "And isn't familiarity better than having to do the pretty with a stranger?" She shrugged. "It's something to think about. I'm not saying you should proposition him merely based on rumors of his prowess, but I *am* saying that if he comes your way during a society event that you keep an open mind."

"Pish posh, Tabby. I wouldn't feel comfortable with that sort of thing and him. He will always be my brother's best friend and nothing else." Thinking about him in such a capacity was simply silly, wasn't it? "Besides, I haven't seen him since before I was married. We barely have a connection any longer."

"All of that is true, of course, but who knows what can happen. May Day is rapidly approaching, and magic can occur at that time of year."

Though she loved Tabetha's whimsy, she rather thought she'd long outgrown such things, and the viscount wasn't someone she'd ever thought about in romantic or carnal ways. She needed a much different man than someone who buzzed from flower to flower, for she'd already had a man who'd cared nothing for her.

Never again.

CHAPTER THREE

April 25, 1817
Trentmore House
St. James's Place
Mayfair, London

WHY THE DEVIL *do I continue coming to these events?*

Once more, Nathaniel was cooling his heels at yet another rout in Mayfair. While he'd chatted with friends and exchanged greetings with a few acquaintances, there was absolutely nothing to hold his interest.

Of course, there'd been delightful discussions on issues of the day, and he usually adored joining in a spirited debate, but for whatever reason, he suffered heavily from ennui. Nothing seemed to spark enthusiasm in him, and he couldn't quite put a finger on it.

To be fair, things would have been better if his best friend had come with him, but since William wished to hover about his parents' home for obvious reasons, Nathaniel was on his own. If he were a decent sort, he'd attend to the duties of his title and make inroads into charming his way through the petticoat line, especially since more than a few ladies were casting calf-eyed gazes at him. However, the thought of hooking the notice of an innocent—cheeky or otherwise—left him with a bad taste in his mouth after what had occurred three nights ago.

With the shake of his head, he slowly left the drawing room

in pursuit of something more erudite or exciting. Hopefully, either could be found within the townhouse; otherwise, he'd simply remove to his own to save him from being killed by dullness.

Humming a rambling bit of a tuneless song, Nathaniel made his way down to the lower level. Though there were a few people meandering the corridor outside the library, he hoped they didn't wish to linger in the room itself, for he wasn't in the mood to be social. Which was quite odd because usually he worked the room as if he were a politician. Tonight, though, he couldn't summon enough wherewithal for all that.

What is wrong with me?

Perhaps too many things pressed in upon him right now, so when he stepped into the library, the atmosphere inside was quite pleasant as he let himself accustom to the quiet and the dimly lit interior. It was a rainy night outside, and someone had pushed one of the windows slightly open to admit the unique scent of petrichor. God, that was one of the best fragrances, and one of the most underrated. A handful of candles were lit about the room, but the illumination was such that they left shadows clinging to the ceiling and into the corners, leaving behind the mysterious feel from the rain outside.

When he came further into the room, he frowned as his gaze fell onto a woman who occupied one of the leather wingback chairs. She had a book in her hand, and she held it fairly close to her face, perhaps because she might not be able to read words close without reading spectacles.

Was she vain or had she merely forgotten to bring them, not figuring she'd need them during a society event?

Interesting, that. Then an elusive combination of scents teased his nose—rose, perhaps a splash of citrus, and a hint of something sweet like vanilla but not quite that. It drew him toward the woman in an effort to identify the notes. Threads of silver glimmered in her black hair in the low light, and those tresses had been arranged in a simple chignon with the curls twisted and gathered behind her head by a duo of crushed-diamond-encrusted combs.

"I beg your pardon. I don't wish to disturb your reading enjoyment, but I find your perfume quite alluring." At least it wasn't a lie.

"Oh, thank you." When the lady glanced up at him, he was immediately taken aback by the dark sapphire pools of her eyes; he'd seen them before. Of course he had, for they were the same as his best friend, William.

Shit!

Was this his older sister? "Never say you're Lady Diana Sammerson?"

A pleased smile curved her lips that were neither thin nor full. "Well, I was once upon a time. I'm Lady Diana Woodbine currently, or the Dowager Lady Atterbury, if you'd rather."

He snorted. "No one who is as lovely as you should ever be referred to as *dowager*." Flirting came as natural to him as breathing.

"Ha. Thank you for that." Then her eyes widened as she took in his face, moved her gaze up and down his person. "Lord Holdcraft, Nathaniel Grossbeck?"

"In the flesh."

"Good heavens, it's been an age since I've seen you!" Genuine pleasure infused her tone.

Though it was difficult to study the whole of her form due to her sitting in that leather chair, her gown of raspberry silk was the exact shade to bring life to her pale skin. The color put him in mind of spring flowers, and paired with the enticing scent, he could easily envision her walking in gardens somewhere, bending to smell a spring bloom. And with the teasing band of thin lace around the low, rounded bodice as well as the bottom of the short, puffed sleeves, she was everything feminine and delicate.

What sort of a woman had she grown into? And was she the same woman now that she'd been when she'd married Atterbury?

"Indeed." How serendipitous. She was just the thing he needed to bring interest back to the evening. Excitement buzzed at the base of his spine. "It is good to see you again. I'd no idea you had returned to London, but William said he expected you soon."

"That is quite true." A bit of sadness shadowed her eyes. "I did, indeed, come in anticipation of my father's impending death. Unfortunately, Papa is clinging to this mortal coil, but we expect him to let go at any time. It is merely a matter of waiting." She had a much more descriptive way of saying that than William had.

"You have my condolences all the same. I remember your father as a man who loved the out of doors, and he embraced his role of earl with joy." That was something he'd envied about her father. "Sometimes it is hell growing older. For many reasons, but one of the worst is the fact we begin to lose the people that we love."

She nodded. "It rather is."

"Oh, and belated condolences for the loss of your husband."

"There is no need." The lady waved away his comment. "As we grow older, we also lose those we didn't really love at all as well."

Yes, clearly, she was a different woman. Another tidbit of interest that he tucked away to comment upon at a later date. "I see." Oddly, wanting to prolong the unexpected meeting, he asked gestured to the book she still held. "What are you reading this evening?"

"Poetry from Burns. There is something about it I adore." When she met his gaze again, her eyes twinkled in the dim illumination. "There is so much imagery involved, so much hope and struggle, when he talks about the overcoming of such or even love…" She shook her head. "I'll admit, my heart gives a little flutter."

How charming. "That's what I think as well, with the exception of the fluttering heart." Daring much, he gave her a wink. "Poetry is something of a hobby of mine." How easy it was to converse with her. Was that due to the fact he'd known her long ago or a testament to the woman herself?

Surprise entered her expression. "Do you write it? I never heard my brother say that about you."

An unexpected chuckle pulled from his throat. "I do not. It seems I haven't either the courage to set pen to paper or a compelling enough subject. So I spend my time reading others' work, and have been quite happy to do so."

Though seeing Diana again was a good start. Perhaps an ode to her lips was in order.

"I understand that. As much as I might wish to try my hand at writing poetry—or even prose—I wouldn't know where to start." The way she moved her hands, the fact that she had a habit of tilting her head ever so slightly to the side when she talked, the intentional inflections of her voice, how deep blue her eyes were all worked to prove captivating.

"It is difficult, this wavering on the edge and not knowing what to do, but I'm hoping I'll find a subject to inspire me more sooner rather than later."

The lady nodded even as she frowned, and he couldn't stop himself from dropping his gaze to her mouth. "What are you doing down here? I assume you are a guest for the rout. Why aren't you mingling? Especially since popular gossip holds that you always have a new woman on your arm each week."

One of his eyebrows rose. "Why aren't you?"

"Touché." Lady Diana allowed a slight smile, and he wished it were full so he could see the whole effect. "As much as I want to reenter society and perhaps put myself back into circulation, I found I wasn't prepared for the noise or the crowds. Or even how the younger set act much differently than I did at their age." A string of laughter escaped her throat, and it was just as captivating as the rest of her. "I fear it will take a few outings to acclimate myself to the changes society has seen since I was last mired in it."

"That is a good observation, though. The young ladies these days border on bold and fast. They'd rather leave nothing to the imagination." However, this lady was far too fascinating to merely leave her in peace. "Do you mind company?"

"Of course not. We can catch up. There are twenty plus years since we've seen each other, and much has happened within those years, I'll wager."

"Indeed, and in your case, it seems as if those years has made you into a mysterious widow with stories to tell." With a nodcock idea in his head, Nathaniel strode to the door and softly closed it, making certain he locked it before joining her at the grouping of furniture. "And in my case, I'm afraid the time has passed, and it hasn't made me any better than I've ever been."

What a sad commentary on my life.

"I doubt that's true." She shrugged. "But for me, I married, bore two children who have grown into lovely adults, and then survived my husband's death. In the middle of all that?" A sigh escaped her. "There was living, I suppose, tending to other peoples' needs, and when I finally had the time to catch my breath, I found I was alone at sixes and sevens with *my* needs mostly unmet."

"Mmm, succinct story, but there is a wealth of important things you've left out. I understand why." What did she need in this moment? Drifting toward her chair, he continued. "Over those years, I lost my father to an attack of his heart. A few years later, my mother died from complications of an infection her body just couldn't fight." God, those had been terrible years. "Each death changes the people who are left behind. I knocked about Town with your brother for a good portion of that time."

"Avoiding the responsibilities of your title?"

"Perhaps, but I'd rather marry with intention than be trapped with someone dreadfully wrong for me and then grow to regret it."

"That is so true, and you're smart to follow that advice." Her expression sobered. "I wish I'd done the same."

"Mmm." How interesting that she'd come back into his life right now, for he had been mildly attracted to her years before when she was a younger woman, just after she'd said vows to

Atterbury. She'd been the catch of the Season that year, and the whole of the *ton* buzzed about her match, but he'd thought, personally, they weren't suited for each other. And he'd said as much to William, who'd ignored him. The memory tugged a chuckle from his throat.

"What is so funny?"

It wouldn't hurt to admit that since it was such a long time ago. "I was attracted to you just after you married. The folly of a randy eighteen-year-old young man, I suppose."

"I never knew that." Surprise jumped into her eyes. "I was a bride of three and twenty. The engagement, if you can call it that, was a whirlwind. I was packed up and handed over to my husband from my father."

"I told your brother that Atterbury didn't deserve you."

"What did he say?"

"He said the marriage was what your father wanted, that he gained a choice property in the Lake District from the contracts."

She nodded. "He did, and I never had the chance to visit it, but I hear it's beautiful in the summer." A few seconds later, she pressed her lips together. "Why didn't you say anything to me about your feelings at the time?"

"What good would it have done? I was a green boy, a nod-cock, and you were married." He shrugged. "William would have killed me, besides. He wanted me to court your younger sister. Said we would have been perfect for each other."

"William often can't see past the end of his nose." Another laugh left her throat. "A match between you and my sister would have gone nowhere. She has always been in love with the man she married. In fact, she announced at the age of fifteen that she'd marry him and have a large family with him, which she has. And from what I hear, she's still mad for him to this day."

"A romance like that is something I aspire to. My parents didn't have that; they were constantly fighting, much more so after my sister died in her childhood." Another truth. He just assumed he would never have a loving union, which was why he continually sought out shallow liaisons. They were easier, and he didn't need to work at them.

And most of the time, they didn't prove a disappointment.

She nodded. "There is a certain comfort in familiarity." Again, she roved her bright gaze up and down his form with an accuracy that he could almost feel.

Did such familiarity translate to the resurrection of attraction or desire brewing between them now? "What do you wish you had now, Lady Diana?"

"Just Diana. I don't need to be reminded of my title."

"No, I don't suppose you do." With even more daring, Nathaniel moved in front of her chair, gripped the armrests, and then leaned into her, watching her the whole time. "But that didn't answer my question."

Her eyelids fluttered. "What do I want? I'm not certain yet."

"Then what do you need?" he asked next since it mirrored his earlier thoughts.

"Another impossible question to answer on the spot." But curiosity lit her eyes.

"Ah, so you won't mind if I did this, hmm?" Then, because he might have lost his mind, he claimed her lips with his, kissing her gently.

He eased away slightly. Would she slap him? She very nearly did, as one of her hands rose and surprise again moved across her face. Then she frowned and shadows filled her eyes. "Why did you do that?"

"Why not?" There was nothing to do but shrug. "I wanted to."

"But… why? I'm not looking to be the next in the long line of conquests you have."

Fair enough. He held her gaze. "To see if I was only remembering that old attraction from when I was an idiot of eighteen, or if something new and interesting is building between us."

A slight hitch of her breathing betrayed her curiosity. "And?"

"It is quite valid and strong."

Diana's eyes widened. "Fascinating."

"Indeed." For the space of a few heartbeats, they stared at each other. "What now?" This was a delicate and developing situation, so he didn't wish to ruin anything by rushing forward.

"Hmm." Slowly, and with determined movements, she set her book onto a small table nearby and then stood, which put her immediately into his arms as he straightened. "I think you should kiss me again to be certain."

How delightfully unexpected. If she hadn't looked at him with the same hunger in her expressive eyes that was currently coursing through his blood, if her fingers hadn't curled into the lapel of his tailcoat, if the tip of her tongue hadn't darted out to moisten her bottom lip, he would have been fine. He could have potentially bid her goodnight and returned to the drawing room, content with reconnecting with an old acquaintance, but all those things *had* happened, and his world tilted.

"I might be many things, but a disappointment to a lady when a kiss is in the offing is not one of them."

With a groan, Nathaniel wrapped her more securely in his arms and crushed his lips to hers, only this time, he didn't keep it chaste—couldn't. This was everything he'd dreamed of as a youth of eighteen. He wanted much more from her than he could articulate with words, for this embrace should never have happened. Yet... She tasted so sweet, felt like walking into a warm house from a cold snowstorm. When he encouraged her lips to part, she gasped, and he took full advantage. The second his tongue slid against hers, another portion of his control shattered.

Apparently not to be outdone, Diana kissed him back with an enthusiasm that matched his own. Satin slid over steel as they dueled for control, but when finally she surrendered to him with a tiny sigh, need shivered down his spine. She encircled his shoulders with her arms, and the second her fingers caressed his nape, common sense fled.

Christ, this is so much better than dallying with debutantes.

While devouring her mouth as if he were a man starving, Nathaniel lifted her off the floor, shuttled her along the hardwood and carpeting, and at a half-moon-shaped table in front of a shelf, he deposited her arse onto the piece of furniture. A couple of books that had been piled on the surface tumbled to the floor with dull thumps and thuds, but he didn't care. Not when kissing Diana had suddenly brought an extra spice to his life, and made him forget he'd ever been bored tonight.

The pounding of his pulse in his ears kept time to the insistent throb of his shaft as he dragged his lips along the column of her silky neck. That faint floral and sweet scent she wore was both demure and naughty. It spurred him onward, beckoned him closer until he held her head in his palms and moved between her naturally splayed legs.

"Nathaniel, I..." She didn't finish the sentence, for he returned to her lips as if he couldn't bear to be parted from them. Hell, in many ways, he'd waited two and twenty years for this chance. A soft sound of pleasure came from her throat, and damn if he didn't wish to hear that again. She fumbled with his cravat, and apparently abandoning the effort, she surged upward to press her lips to the skin of his throat just above that garment.

"God." Need slammed into him; he was nearly drunk on her and he'd only just met her after such a long absence. The fact she wasn't a shrinking violet nor a desperate widow fanned the flames in his blood. Clearly, there was a spark between them that had the potential to blow into an inferno, but he wasn't one to jump into a romance, didn't know if that was what he wanted anyway, or with her.

But this lady was far too good for a bit of slap and tickle with him walking away directly afterward. What the hell did that leave?

By the time she put a hand to his chest and gave him a bit of a hard shove, he had a raging cockstand and a wave of hot lust slammed through his veins. "Good heavens," she said in a whisper, as she stood peering up at him, for she was a good four inches or so shorter than he.

"Agreed. What now?" Why did he suddenly feel like a green youth when presented with a woman of her caliber?

"Hmm." With a slight smile, Diana patted his cheek and touched her bottom lip with the tip of her tongue as she dropped her gaze briefly to his mouth before holding his gaze once more. "Call on me tomorrow. I'm in Grosvenor Square. Perhaps we can further talk at that time or take a drive to Hyde Park."

What the devil for? "What will that gain us?" He wasn't accustomed to not acting on carnal impulses the moment they occurred.

"Who can say what the future holds, Nathaniel?" Hearing his name in her tone sent shivers into the lusty mix bedeviling him. "But I wonder if you are as skilled at certain *things* as the rumors throughout society say you are." Then, with a wink, she glided across the floor, unlocked the door, and exited the room.

Fuck me and damn me too.

It had been a long time indeed since his world had been turned on its head with one kiss from a woman. Even more so that he'd been knocked stupid by an experienced one.

CHAPTER FOUR

April 26, 1817
Atterbury House
Grosvenor Square
Mayfair, London

As Diana stepped into the morning room around noon the next day, her cheeks were still warm from remembering that kiss she'd shared with Lord Holdcraft last night.

Good heavens, what came over me?

That kiss had taken her by surprise. One moment they'd been catching up on each other's lives through the briefest summaries, and then the next, he'd kissed her. Which had then made her quite brazen, for she'd wasted no time kissing him back, as well as issuing the invitation to call. Why? What had she been thinking?

A snort issued from her as she perched on a delicate chair in one corner of the room. To be honest, she hadn't been thinking, especially once she'd let herself surrender to that kiss. Never in her married life had Atterbury kissed her like that, even while in the throes of alleged passion during the handful of times he'd bedded her. There had been something head-turning and pulse-racing about that kiss with Nathaniel—her brother's best friend— and a man younger than her by five years.

And she'd been immediately intrigued.

Though she'd known of him as a young woman through her brother, she'd not fancied him at that time. He'd been far too immature and ridiculous. How did she think of him now? Oh, that was an easy answer. As she patted a few escaped hair strands back into her chignon, she smiled to herself. Nathaniel Grossbeck was quite delicious from what she'd seen in that quick meeting and even quicker kiss.

And she wanted to know more if only for the experience.

Did that mean for more than just kisses and conversation? That was something she hadn't thought through, but if it did, why chase that with one of the biggest rakes in London? There wouldn't be so much gossip about him if some of it wasn't true. Additionally, she was old enough and experienced enough to know that a few kisses—or anything else—didn't equate to love, but a woman had needs, and there was nothing wrong with having a tryst as a widow to have those needs met.

At least she could have a wild romp or two, and then her mind would be clear so she could tackle the *ton*, perhaps find a decent man who might be searching for a wife. Isn't that what men did? Dally with more interesting women until they found one to wed?

A discreet knock at the open door wrenched Diana from her thoughts.

"Yes, Cartwright?" The butler had been in her husband's employ since she'd married Atterbury, and she didn't have the heart to change the staff. If her son wished to do that, he could at his own discretion.

The tall, thin man with graying brown hair offered a slight bow. "Viscount Holdcraft has come to call. He wishes to speak with you. Are you receiving?"

Her nerves felt strung too tight, for a part of her hadn't truly believed he'd come. "Uh…" Then she cleared her throat and nodded. "I am, yes. Please escort him here."

"Of course, my lady."

Once Cartwright left, she blew out a breath. It had been an age since she'd last been with a man—even before her husband had died—yet she didn't know if that was where today's meeting would end. Still, the wondering was enough to bring out a bit of anxiety.

"Ah, Lady Atterbury. Thank you for seeing me today." In one hand, he carried a bouquet of spring flowers, including lilies and tulips, wrapped in pale-pink paper.

Her stomach dropped at the sound of the viscount's voice as he entered the room. Rising, she inclined her head. "Good afternoon, Holdcraft." When the butler asked if she wanted tea, Diana shook her head. "Not just now. But be assured I'll ring if the viscount or I require anything. We are merely catching up. He is my brother's best friend, and I haven't seen him for over twenty years." Was she trying too hard to seem proper in front of a servant? When nothing untoward had occurred?

"Of course, my lady."

"And Cartwright, please close the door. I don't wish to be disturbed, unless my brother calls."

"Very well." Then the butler once more exited the room.

Tingles of anticipation played her spine when she was left alone with Nathaniel. "I'll admit, part of me didn't believe you would actually follow through and pay me a visit." Good heavens, he smelled so good!

Citrus, sandalwood, and cedar wafted to her nose as he came further into the room and offered her the bouquet. "After the intriguing meeting we had at the rout last night, I was quite interested in continuing our conversation."

The words were disarming enough but they held a double meaning that sent ripples of awareness dancing over her skin. "Ah." When their fingers brushed as she took the bouquet, she tamped down on the urge to give in to a shiver. "Thank you for the flowers. I do so enjoy fresh blooms but rarely ever have them." It pleased her that he'd done such, because her husband hadn't given her gifts since she'd birthed their son. When she'd been delivered of their daughter, he hadn't even been in London and had gone to Brighton with his mistress.

"You are quite welcome. Honestly, I'm not in the habit of

picking up flowers, but as I passed a woman with a handcart on my way here, they were so pretty and put me in mind of you, that I couldn't resist."

So he'd been thinking of her? *Oh, dear.* Heat went through her cheeks, which discomfited her, for wasn't she too old for such things? "Well, they are wonderful, and tulips are my favorite." The pink and white blooms were the very herald of spring. Not knowing what to do, she brought the bouquet to her nose and inhaled the floral aroma. "I hope this visit isn't disrupting your schedule," she said as she moved to the circular table on the other side of the room where she usually took breakfast. It sat four but she rarely had visitors.

"Not at all. And I don't rise before noon for just anyone," he teased, with a wink.

She smiled. "Ah, you're a dissolute lord, then?" Thankfully, an empty vase sat in the middle of the table, for one of the maids usually brought in flowers for tea, so she slipped the bouquet into the vessel. Water could be added later.

"Perhaps, but that would depend on one's perspective." As he paced about the room, peering into curio cabinets and shelves, she took the opportunity to study him.

A strong jaw gave way to slightly chiseled cheekbones, but it was his head full of light-red hair and his moss-green eyes beneath red eyebrows that made her breathless. A smattering of freckles lay sprinkled over his cheeks and the bridge of his nose, and his shoulders were wide and strong. She remembered what it had felt like to have his arms about her and how solid his chest was when he'd been pressed against her.

Would she have the opportunity to see what his body looked like *sans* clothing? Would he let her explore his form with her fingers and mouth?

Then he turned and caught her staring. As another splash of heat went through her cheeks, a slow, sensual grin curved his lips. "Shall I spin about for you so you can observe me from behind? I've been told my arse is quite something to behold."

"Do shut up, Nathaniel." But she couldn't help her own grin. It was too bad she hadn't known him well before she'd married Atterbury. He could have been good fun. That wouldn't have changed the direction of her fate, but she might have been able to face it all the better.

He came closer to the chair she'd perched upon. "I have been friends with your brother for most of my life, and if William hasn't yet cut me loose, you can be sure I'm not a complete scoundrel. However, you already know I'm a rake, so shall we be honest with each other?"

"Of course."

"Then I'll ask you this. Did you enjoy a healthy carnal life with your husband?"

"Oh." Right to the heart of the matter. She avoided his gaze as if there was something wrong with her in *that* scenario. "I did not. He told me time out of hand that he preferred bed sport with his mistress, and that once he had his heir and a spare—or in our case, my daughter—he wouldn't come to my bed again."

Shock went through the viscount's expression. "God, what a bounder." He shook his head. "And he must have been mad, for had he ever looked at you? Not to be crass, but you are quite lovely, even more so now than when I knew you as a young woman."

Was that genuine or was it flattery? Perhaps it didn't matter, for his praise put warmth back into her cheeks. But Diana shrugged. "It happens more than you'd think, and it's quite demoralizing after a while. I'd begun to ask myself what was wrong with me that I couldn't hold my own husband's atten- tion."

"I can just imagine, but the failing was on his part. Not yours. Never think that." Nothing but honesty reflected in his eyes. "Some men don't understand what they have."

She snorted. "While this is true, I'll wager you're just as bad as he was."

Consternation filtered through his expression. "What?"

"Well, you go from woman to woman, getting what you need from them. Not caring if they're satisfied, never letting yourself form attachments or feelings for them. That isn't decent behavior, is it?"

A frown tugged at the corners of his mouth. "That's not all true. I'm *quite* diligent in making certain the women I'm with are satisfied."

"Perhaps that may be so." One of her eyebrows rose. "Why are you a bachelor still at forty? With no close friendships except with my brother, and no women in your life beyond the shallow relationships you cling to?"

That apparently gave him pause, for he crossed his arms at his chest as if trying to protect himself. "I suppose I just haven't found a woman worth pursuing, one with whom I could see a lifetime with."

"Yet rumor has it you need to marry."

"Don't we all at some point?"

She nodded. "Again, perhaps. Do you think you're that sort of man? The marrying kind? The forever kind? Would you be happy with just one woman in your bed for the rest of your life?"

"Honestly? I have no idea." Confusion reflected in his green eyes. "It would largely depend on the woman. However, if such a woman exists to hold my attention past a bedding, I would consider myself beyond intrigued."

Was that a challenge? Regardless, amusement pushed through her chest. "Perhaps you should find out, hmm?"

It was his turn to raise an eyebrow. "Meaning?"

"Start with a kiss and see where the afternoon goes." Diana shrugged. Did such a suggestion brand her a tart, then? This was new territory for her, and crossing verbal swords with her brother's best friend brought a lovely bit of scandal to the conversation.

Surprise flickered over his face. "You are assuming… what?"

"Nothing, of course, for there is free will involved from both parties. I merely want a bit of fun, perhaps a tryst, this afternoon."

Was it too bold to come right out and admit it?

"Oh." Nathaniel looked at her with speculation for the space of a few heartbeats, then finally, he nodded. "Well, let's see what sort of mettle you have, Lady Atterbury."

"Ha. It's Diana and you know it."

"Very well… *Diana*." With desire darkening his eyes, he grabbed one of her hands and drew her into a standing position. "I haven't had a woman challenge me like this in a very long while, and I rather enjoy it."

"Good." She didn't have time to revel in the sound of her name in his deep tenor, for he crushed his mouth on hers in his opening overture.

And it was everything she'd experienced the night before. There was some comfort in the fact that he was exactly as he claimed. With a soft sound of encouragement at the back of her throat, Diana slid her hands up his chest that was indeed surprisingly hard for his age and loosely looped her arms about the breadth of his shoulders. Then she set out to kiss him back.

Why should he have all the fun? After all, she was the one who hinted at this way to spend the time.

Except, the viscount wasn't a rake for nothing. Absolutely, he refused to let her boss him during that kiss. Instead, he settled her more comfortably into his embrace, and then he set out to apparently separate her from her senses. He moved over her lips with slow leisure that would drive her mad before too long, but then, that was exactly what she wanted. When she applied pressure at his nape in a bid to hurry him along, he ignored her and took his time.

Cheeky indeed.

Over and over, he nipped and nibbled her lips in a bid to introduce himself. Soft but firm, those two pieces of flesh both cradled hers and provided enough stimulation and heat that her body felt as if it were vibrating, shifting, preparing for whatever else he had planned. Oh, and she couldn't wait to find out.

How was it that two men's kisses could prove so different and evoke such different reactions in her?

When he drew the tip of his tongue along her lower lip, erotic sensations trailed after, and she gasped from the unexpected delight of it. Not once had she felt the same when Atterbury had attempted an embrace. Holdcraft took advantage of her distraction to slide that organ into her mouth and flirt with her tongue. A game as old as eternity commenced, as they both thrust and parried while the kiss deepened, and time seemed to stand still.

This is what I've been missing my entire life, this intensity, this thrill, this feeling that a man is engulfed with need for... me.

Heady stuff, that. Desire clouded her brain as the heady embrace continued. Good heavens, she craved the heat of him, the feel of him, the sensation of being held by him, and in fact tugged him closer until their bodies were layered scandalously against each other. The scent of him accelerated her heartbeat, and oh she couldn't have enough him.

Eventually, Nathaniel pulled away merely to drag his lips down the side of her neck while her fingers went into his hair. How wonderfully soft and thick it was! Atterbury was nearly bald by the time he popped off this mortal coil. Then he guided those talented lips to the tops of her breasts, and flutters erupted in her lower belly as the glide of his mouth heightened her awareness of him.

"Damnation, you are most intoxicating," he whispered against her skin, but his hands were at her breasts, cupping them, teasing her nipples through the fabric, and sending shivery sensations through her veins. "You are certain you want this?"

"I am, as long as you don't talk to William about it."

Oh, for the love of the gods, put your mouth on me!

The dratted man must have read her mind, for he curled his fingers into the low bodice of her day dress. In a thrice, he pulled the fabric down, taking the chemise with it, and didn't stop until her modest breasts were bared to his inspection. "I knew you would be perfection after seeing you last night in the gown you wore," he murmured seconds before he took one of those aching tips into the warm cavern of his mouth.

"Mmm!" The hiss of approval seemed to hover in the room. Diana arched her back, which put her more firmly into his hold. How long had it been since a man had pleasured her so thoroughly without even putting a hand between her thighs? She stifled the urge to snort. Or rather, in her husband's case, climb on top of her, rut, and then leave? "Goodness, but I feel much like an innocent again."

Was it silly of her to admit?

"Just wait," he whispered around her nipple before moving to the other tip and starting the seduction all over again.

Suckling, soothing with his tongue, and then he withdrew only to blow upon the moisture he'd introduced onto her flesh. It was a heady combination, and already she shook with anticipation for what else was to come.

I've been cheated out of so much!

When he rolled those sensitive peaks, starting at the root and moving upward with varying degrees of pressure, Diana cried out with approval and more than a little need. A chuckle was his only answer, and it got her dander up a bit.

If he wants tit for tat, he'll have it.

Shoving a hand between their bodies while he continued his carnal torture, Diana cupped his impressive erection through the fabric. A groan left his throat, both haunting and arousing, and she smiled. "Did you think you would leave this morning room unbothered, Nathaniel?"

"I don't know what I expected, to be honest, especially from an older woman."

"Age has nothing to do with pleasure." She stroked him as best she could through his breeches. Oh, he was so impossibly hard that she couldn't wait to see him, touch him, taste him. Where this man was concerned, she had apparently gone temporarily mad.

Perhaps that wasn't a bad thing, for she'd been deprived of such for far too long.

"Fuck." His guttural utterance sent gooseflesh over her skin. Leaving off with his own teasing, the viscount yanked her hand from his person. "Shall we move on to other explorations, then?"

Was she really doing this? The insane flutter of her heartbeat said she was, so she nodded. "Before we do anything more than kissing, I need to know you are not carrying any sort of disease." It ran against arousal, but she refused to put her health at risk, and from his own admission, he wasn't exactly chaste.

His chuckle loosed butterflies in her belly. "I'm pleased you are so shrewd." But he nodded. "I have, in fact, seen my personal physician just last month. I am quite healthy. In the event you wondered, I am selective with the women I take into my bed."

"Surprising, but good to know." However, even upper-class courtesans could carry disease.

He lowered his voice. "Dying of syphilis is not a life goal. Neither is contracting lice or any other sort of crawly thing. I have standards, after all."

For whatever reason, that struck her as funny. A giggle left her throat. "I suppose we can resume."

With a half growl, half curse, he put a hand to the small of her back. "No more Holdcraft nonsense. I'm Nathaniel. Or you can refer to me as a god, once I'm finished with you," he said, with a wink.

What an ego this one had! Yet heated tingles raced down her spine. "You are quite full of yourself."

"And so you will be too, if things progress. Should we lock the door or any other connecting ones?"

"We shouldn't be interrupted." She frowned. Why must he talk about that right now? Why couldn't they return to erotic banter?

"You're certain? I will not wish to be denied once I have your skirts rucked up."

Merciful heavens. She shivered as cool ambient air wafted over her breasts, which still hung out of her gown. It was both scandalous and arousing. "My staff knows how to follow orders."

As long as her brother and her son didn't both decide to come calling, they would be fine. Then Nathaniel caught her in a loose embrace, walked her ahead of him until a brocade wingback chair hit the backs of her knees. She tumbled into that piece of furniture with a squeak of surprise.

"There is nothing more seductive than a woman in any form of undress with passion flushing her cheeks." Appreciation glittered in his eyes as his gaze roved over her form.

"Ha! Don't try to charm me, for I have already given you permission." Diana was nearly drunk on the desire flooding her veins and filling her head. A tryst with him was exactly what she needed, and wanting to further tease him, she slowly pulled up her skirting, hooked a knee on the chair arm, and met his gaze. One of her eyebrows quirked upward. "Why is it I am still waiting to find out if you are as good as the gossips say?"

"Minx." A groan left his throat as he kneeled in front of the chair. The moment he touched her legs and pulled her toward him, tingles of need flew down her spine. "I do so adore a woman who knows exactly what she wants."

"Well, I knew that all the years of my marriage, but that didn't matter. I never received it." She rested a knee over his shoulder.

"You will today, and in that, you have my word." He wasted no time in shoving her skirting up to her waist. Then his fingers were on that private part of her, spreading her open, and she waited with held breath, for her husband had rarely pleasured her in this manner. "I'll wager you need some very *specific* attention now."

No matter that she wished to give him a retort, the second he licked her flesh, the words evaporated from her mind like mist before the sun. All too soon, he encouraged that tiny pearl out of hiding—for she was already semi-aroused from his earlier teasing—and with each probe and flick of his tongue, it swelled and grew more sensitive.

"I..." Diana dug her fingernails into the brocade of the chair's arms. The way Nathaniel moved over her button, the way he worried the nub, suckled at it, gave it little nibbles... It was both extraordinary and foreign. So much so that she squirmed in the chair in an attempt to elude his hold, but the viscount was having none of it.

"If you run away, I can't meet all your needs," he whispered against her flesh, then soothed the throbbing bud with his tongue.

Diana panted. She thrashed her head from side to side as pressure built and stacked in her lower belly. "It's so different... I must be drowning because I never knew..." Intense sensations crashed over her, had enough force to make her faint. She moved a hand to the back of his head, holding him to where she needed him to be. "More."

His chuckle added heightened awareness to his ministrations, but he did as bid. The cheeky man added fingers to his play, sliding them in and out of her quivering passage, and that slow, languid rhythm bumped against the concentrated attention he paid to that button.

"Goodness me..."

As he applied enough friction to drive her mad, Diana's body stiffened, and with a surprised sort of scream, she went over the edge. Or more to the point, she was tossed over and careened into the air where she pinwheeled into a void filled with shimmering light. Her body shook; her core rocked with contractions. It was all she could do to ride the waves.

For the first time in years, she hit release with a man instead of by her own fingers, and this was so much better!

"Dear heavens." She collapsed into the chair and stared at him—sated and winded. "I suppose I must admit to your skill."

Nathaniel chuckled. The sound sent renewed flutters of awareness down her spine. "I'm glad I could be of service."

"Yes, you are *exactly* what I need right now," she managed to whisper.

"God, you are quite the picture." He tugged a handkerchief from his waistcoat pocket and proceeded to wipe the moisture from his face. A supremely smug grin curved his lips. "How was that for an audition?"

"For what?" Good heavens, she could hardly think. She patted a sweat-damp curl back into her chignon.

"Anything? Everything?" His shrug was elegantly negligent. "An affair. It doesn't need to be long or drawn out. We both have certain… urges. There is attraction and desire between us. We get on together." After he was done with the handkerchief, he passed it on to her. "Why shouldn't we have a bit of fun until we both find other interests?"

Goodness, he mentioned an affair before she could. How… interesting. However, though he'd satisfied her initial curiosity, she wasn't looking for an affair. She wanted something more permanent… but she supposed it wouldn't hurt to play with him for a bit until she found someone who could fill a husband role. A younger man with energy and the drive for carnal games was nothing to sneeze at. "When shall we start?"

"Haven't we already done that?" He winked. "From the looks of things, you hit release quite violently."

"It's not well done of you to mention it." Oh, he would be trouble, yet he made her feel younger than her years. She quickly used the handkerchief to wipe between her legs the best she could while she grinned. "Do you want to stay? Go driving?"

"Or continue this?" He raked his hungry gaze over her body. "As much as I would adore that, I have a meeting with my man of affairs this afternoon. Shall we meet tomorrow?"

This was happening so quickly, but oddly, she welcomed it. After years of neglect and doing everything for others, this was her time. "Yes. Come collect me around noon. We'll drive to Hyde Park. I'd like to do some walking if the weather is fair." When she folded the handkerchief, he took it from her, tucked it away. "Also, I'd like to make a call on an acquaintance of mine with a large library. I'm looking for a particular book."

"Very well." He nodded. "I'll see you tomorrow." With another expression of male smugness, he left the room and Diana collapsed onto the chair with a longing in her belly for another form of satisfaction altogether.

What have I just agreed to?

CHAPTER FIVE

April 27, 1817
Hyde Park

EXHILARATION MOVED THROUGH Nathaniel's body as he guided his horse over the bridle paths in Hyde Park. Though morning rides weren't as free or uninhibited in London like they were in the country, still, nothing compared to being in the saddle of a favorite mount and breathing in the crisp, spring morning air.

Though he would be here again later in the day with Diana, he couldn't pass on the opportunity to take in the exercise. He enjoyed it, and since the events of yesterday afternoon, he had pent up energy as well as desire circling through his veins.

Damn, but bringing Diana to release, just beginning to explore her body to discover how she liked to be touched and caressed, tasting her delicate flesh... A shiver of need rippled down his spine. That had been unexpectedly arousing and satisfying. Even more so because she hadn't been properly pleasured or even looked after while she'd been married.

Knowing Atterbury had been an idiot of the first order made Nathaniel unaccountably annoyed. He'd been married to that delightful woman for twenty-two years, and in that time, he'd preferred bedding his mistress? It was unfathomable. The viscountess was an empty vessel, hungry to be filled with carnal experience. How could her husband overlook such a boon?

Shoving the thoughts away, he concentrated on the feel of

the leather reins in his hands, the bunch and release of the horse's muscles against his legs, the scent of the earth and growing things on the morning air. He needed a distraction, and quickly, else Diana would consume his mind.

Yet… had she truly agreed to an affair? He needed more information and clarity.

Then he gave himself over to the joy gained from riding through the park until he was interrupted by the sound of his name being hailed.

"Holdcraft!"

Nathaniel tugged on the reins to slow his mount as William came riding abreast of him on his own horse. "I didn't expect you'd be out so early," he said by way of greeting.

His best friend grunted. "Ten o'clock is hardly early."

"Yet you don't usually rise before noon after society events. Did you not attend a ball last night?" He'd been invited but chose not to go, for after being with Diana that afternoon, he didn't have an appetite for what was lurking in society. What was more, now that he'd spent time with Diana, he could more see the similarities between siblings in William.

"I did, but I didn't see you there."

"Because I chose not to attend." When his mount danced with impatience, he tightened his hold on the reins.

"Ah." William frowned. He lifted a hand to adjust how his top hat sat on his light-brown hair. "I wondered where you've been for the past couple of days. It's been odd prowling about social events without you by my side."

Bloody hell.

Nathaniel shrugged. "I have been uncommonly busy."

With a grunt, William peered into his face. "By the by, you seem different."

Knots pulled in his gut. "How so? I can assure you, I'm quite the same man I've always been."

"In small ways, I suppose. Perhaps how you hold yourself?" William flicked his gaze over Nathaniel's face. "I'll wager you have a new woman in your life. Have you taken a mistress?"

Shit, shit, shit.

"Not exactly." What to tell him? It could never be the truth. "Or at least not yet." How would he feel if he knew that Nathaniel might ask his sister to fill that role? Except he suspected that Diana was far too good for that.

William frowned. "Then what happened to keep you from attending various society functions? Hell, you've been absent from the club for the past few evenings, and that's not like you at all."

Since when had his movements been studied so closely by his best friend. But then, they were very much like brothers. Striving for calm, he said, "There *was* a bit of slap and tickle with a woman yesterday. I truly believe she wanted to see what my skill level was." That was at least true. "I hope my performance was good enough."

"Oh ho!" The other man hooted with laughter. "Then you *do* want a mistress but feel she's too good for you." Another laugh escaped. "She either must be highly talented in carnal affairs or higher up in society than you. I've never known you to have your confidence shaken."

"I'm not certain it's been shaken. Perhaps my ego has been smacked, though." He ignored the heat creeping up the back of his neck. "It will prove interesting to see what happens in the coming days." And God help him, William would never know.

"Well, I wish you luck. Far too many women who aspire to be mistresses only want the gifts and free things bestowed upon them by their protectors." The soon-to-be earl shook his head. "It leaves a bad taste in one's mouth."

"True, but I'm quite certain that is not the case here." At least he hoped.

William nodded. "Then you've postponed the need to marry for your title?"

"For the time being. I'd like to enjoy this new lady for a few months." Quite frankly, looked forward to bedding the enticing widow. After that, he would have a more detailed path.

"I understand that all too well, and in many ways, I envy you." A sigh escaped William. "I've no time to devote to a mistress just now."

Immediately, Nathaniel sobered. "To that end, how is your father?"

Sadness shadowed his friend's eyes. "He is declining. No doubt his passing won't be far off." For a few moments, he remained silent before speaking again. "Regardless, I have dinner with my sisters and mother tonight so we can discuss final arrangements."

Which meant his own meeting with Diana couldn't expand since she already had plans. But he nodded. "I'm sorry, William. If you need me for moral support or anything else, I'll be around."

"I appreciate that, and will probably need you more sooner than later."

Hyde Park later that afternoon

DAMN, THERE WAS something... comforting about strolling through the park with Diana by his side. Every little bloom and unfurling leaf on the trees and bushes was far too clear. Had his vision always been like that or had he never paid attention?

"I adore Hyde Park year-round, but I think the spring is my favorite," she said as she flashed him a smile.

Though the bonnet trimmed with satin ribbon in varying shades of pink as well as sprigs of pink silk rosebuds did nothing for the aesthetic of her walking dress and spencer of ivory and pink, the shallow brim did frame her face, and with curls peeking over her forehead, she made quite the charming picture.

"Is it because everything is new and gentle and the winter is finally over?"

"Mmm, perhaps, but it's also because this part of the earth is experiencing a great awakening, as if it remembered there was still life to be had after being dormant for so long." She waved a hand. "I feel a certain synchrony in that, for it is much like I am."

Did she mean carnally? Interesting, even if she didn't. Since he didn't know, Nathaniel nodded. "Understandable." He caught her hand and threaded it through his crooked elbow. "Did you find the book you spoke of before?"

"I did not. Unfortunately, I don't believe any such thing exists, but I'll keep searching. There are other lending libraries I can either visit or write to."

He frowned. "Which book in particular are you searching for? Perhaps I can help."

A giggle left her throat. He didn't know why, but he wished to hear that melodious sound again. "I suspect you already know, since it's a compendium of Keats's work."

Shock moved through his chest. "How did you know I wanted such a thing?"

"My cousin Tabetha has many connections throughout Town. One of them told her of the request, and she passed it along to me since I'm a patron of some of the lending libraries in the area."

"How lovely. I hadn't considered that before, but if you'd like, I can help with the search." Suddenly, that appealed to him very much. "I admire Keats's work, but then, any poetry will have my heart. I find it fascinating."

"You should truly try to write it yourself."

Nathaniel shook his head. "Perhaps sometime." Though he suspected if he spent much more time in her company, he just might. "From the hints you've already given me, I trust your marriage was loveless?" He cleared his throat. "I mean, not to change the subject, but it's bothered me since you introduced it."

"I can imagine." When she shrugged, her shoulder brushed his. Awareness shivered over him. "And it was. I didn't want my union to be that, but I think it was doomed from the start."

"How so?"

"Well, the first few years, I thought we might have had at least the basic of love or even affection, but he was only pretending until I fell pregnant the first time." When she glanced up into his face and met his gaze, shadows reflected in her sapphire eyes. "More often than not, Atterbury wasn't even at the London townhouse with me or the hall in Surrey. He preferred being with his mistress. Eventually, I preferred that scenario to his actually being underfoot or us being together."

The explanation was said with an air of being rehearsed or spoken far too many times.

"That's quite sad." He patted her hand that rested on his arm. "I'm not exactly aligned with the idea of marriage myself, but if I *did* wed, my attention would be fully on my wife." Especially if said woman was as enchanting as the one walking with him now.

"So you say, but reality is much different." For the space of a few heartbeats, she remained quiet. "Do you have a mistress currently?"

"I do not." It was an easy enough question to answer.

"No wonder you go from bed to bed like a sexually depraved honeybee."

"Deflowering virgins and bedeviling widows?" He snorted when she giggled again. "I haven't been that for the past few weeks." Which was odd, but then, he had been suffering from ennui. "The last time I was, we, ah, well we didn't do the deed. She merely serviced my, uh..."

God, how embarrassing.

"Do hush, Nathaniel. You're making it worse." A faint blush stained her cheeks. "Did you whisk her off to a shadowy corner somewhere?"

"Uh..." He tugged at his suddenly too tight cravat with his free hand. "Not exactly. She, uh, led me out of the house and into the square beyond the rear garden."

"Quite bold."

"It was, considering she couldn't have been more than two and twenty, and in the end, she only wished for the title. No doubt wanted to bring me up to scratch by crying scandal." Had she tried the same with someone else?

"Hmph."

Silence brewed between them as they walked deeper into the park, far off the bridle path, and into the trees near a hedgerow. The spring greenery was nearly fully grown in while leaves were bursting on the tree branches. New grass cushioned their footfalls.

"Where are we going?"

"Never say you've explored the park beyond the paths?"

"Rarely."

"Then here is an opportunity to expand your horizons," she said on the heels of a laugh. "I'm taking you to one of my favorite spots."

How intriguing, but she had been that since they'd first met. "Oh?"

She nodded. "I used to come here when I was at low points in my marriage. It felt safe and secure. Sometimes I would bring a tattered blanket out on the grass and sit with a book." The hand resting on his arm trembled. "I'm glad it's still relatively unmolested. I haven't been in London for a few years. There was simply no point in it."

"You didn't wish to visit friends or family?"

"To be honest, after what I'd gone through with Atterbury and making sure the children reached adulthood the best they could, I was tired, and perhaps embarrassed. I didn't want to face anyone I knew if I could help it."

How interesting. "I can understand that, and it irks me that Atterbury put you into that position." Then another thought occurred to him. "Do your children know?"

"I waited until after he died before I revealed anything of that nature, for I didn't want their views of their father destroyed or twisted."

Which meant they probably suspected. He nodded but kept his own counsel as they reached a small clearing that was halfway ringed with evergreens. A pond waited nearby with a handful of ducks floating about the surface. There was a fallen tree that probably served as a seat where she used for reflection. Truly, it was a quaint area.

"I can see why you like it there. It's peaceful and quiet."

She nodded. "It's better than the country at times." Then Diana tugged him into the trees. Once she'd positioned him in front of that stand, she further surprised him by dropping to her knees after moving her skirting out of the way so it wouldn't stain. Only then did she reach for his front falls.

"What the hell?" When he attempted to back away, she held onto the waist of his breeches. "What are you doing?"

Her eyes glittered as she glanced upward and met his gaze. "I'm returning the favor from yesterday."

Another wave of shock slammed into him even as anticipation twisted down his spine. "To see how I find *your* skills?"

A giggle was his reward, and he thought he might be a happy man if he could hear that sound for the rest of his life. "It's only fair, don't you think?" she said with a cheeky grin curving her highly kissable lips.

"Are you one of those wicked widows, then?" God, how lovely would that be?

"We shall discover that together, hmm?" As she spoke, she manipulated the buttons of his front falls, and when his semi-hard length tumbled out, he shivered as the cool, spring air wafted over his flesh. She tsked her tongue. "You are far too tense, Nathaniel. Let me help with that." Before he could protest, she began to tease and caress her fingers along his shaft, encouraging that appendage to grow into a full erection.

"You make me want to throw every caution to the wind," she said in a whisper while she worked.

"Then don't stop." When he reached for her with a wink, she batted his hand away.

"Oh, I don't plan to until you are well and truly sated." With a tiny grin, she continued to manipulate his shaft. Slowly, it hardened and elongated.

A grunt sailed from his throat even as excitement twisted up his spine. "Why, Lady Diana, how scandalous." The fact anyone might come upon them at any moment added a delicious intensity to the imminent act.

"After not being able to act as I wished with Atterbury, I am reveling in the freedom now." She frowned but kept her concentration on his thickening member. "When I met you, it was as if you put a match to dry tinder."

With her fingers wrapped lightly around his shaft, he tried to remain still, but it was quite difficult, for her touch set fire to his blood. "I very much wish to rouse Atterbury from the dead merely for the joy of killing him myself for how he treated you." Where had such a sentiment come from?

"That is sweet, but I'm quite content having him beneath the ground."

As his aroused member grew, he widened his stance so she would have more room to work. "Knowing a woman enjoys a coupling is one of the greatest compliments of the act, and if a man can send her flying, even more so."

"I agree, and now I intend to explore... everything." Diana caressed her fingers up and down the inside of his splayed thighs.

Shivers chased themselves over his skin. If someone were to accidentally ride by or walk over and discover them thusly, there would be hell to pay, but there was nothing for it, and he couldn't wait to see what she would do next.

"I haven't bid you nay." The answer was a tad breathless, for she'd begun to caress the underside of his shaft.

"Then let's start." She sent him a wink before she settled into her task.

Bemused, he stared down at her, and wanting to see her face, he tugged on the satin ribbons beneath her chin. When the bonnet tumbled to the soft grass with a dull thud, he grinned. "Much better. I want to see what you're doing to me." For watching was part of the act, and already, he was randy as hell.

"Cheeky."

"Hmph." The more she handled his equipage, the tighter and longer his length grew. "God…" It wasn't like him to want to spend before things reached their peak.

Diana curled her fingers around him; his girth fit well in her palm. As she experimented with various degrees of pressure, moans escaped him. There was something different and intriguing at how she handled him. It wasn't like the last act he'd experienced. While she kept her gaze on his, she fondled his stones, squeezing and releasing, finding a rhythm she liked that incorporated both them and his length to bring him maximum pleasure.

Fuck me. I won't last. "Where did you learn how to do this?" Emotion graveled his inquiry and he rested a hand on her shoulder.

"Truthfully?"

"Yes." Dear God, it took all his willpower not to spend immediately.

"I spied on the servants a couple of times, then I practiced on a phallus I fashioned with fabric stuffed with dried peas." She shrugged but didn't break her concentration. "I hoped I might marry again one day to a man better suited to me and my inclinations." Her eyes glittered. "Am I doing it correctly?"

"Shit, yes." Nathaniel's respect and admiration for how her mind worked continued to climb. "I… Oh." A moan swallowed whatever else he would have said.

She snorted. "I've only just started." Then she held his gaze as she moved closer to his body. When she licked the wide head of his member, he hissed in warning, yet she took his hardened length into her the warm cavern of her mouth.

And he thought he might die. One of his hands curled into a fist and then relaxed when she eased off. As she bobbed on his member he groaned. "Do you enjoy doing… this?"

"Since this is the first time I'm performing this act on a real man, I would say that I do." The way she grinned as she spoke tightened his chest, for she impressed him with each day that went by. Returning to her work, she swirled her tongue around the underside of his head and added caresses and squeezes to how she pleasured him with her mouth.

His moans came more quickly. Eventually, he couldn't stand it any longer. Holding her head between his hands, Nathaniel slowly thrust, which sent his shaft deeper until the tip hit the back of her throat. She paused, briefly, to no doubt consider if she liked it, then seconds later, she swallowed. When the muscles of her throat gently massaged his member, the sensations that followed were amazing and quite unexpected.

"Good God," he breathed, and his hands went into her hair, fisting and tangling the length while tugging out the pins. After the mass fell about her shoulders, one of his hands cradled her skull. The silver strands that mixed with the light-brown tresses were beautiful in the sunlight that peeked through their semi-private hideaway. "I won't last if you continue."

She chuckled, but she didn't decrease her rhythm. The vibrations around his prick added to the urgency throbbing through his shaft.

"Nearly gone." His whisper was choked as he thrust more forcefully into her mouth. Watching her swollen lips move along his member, feeling the sensations as she worked him over with her tongue and fingers was beyond everything he'd known in recent years.

"Diana, damn..." The more he stroked, the more she used her fingers to heighten that delicious tension. She manipulated his stones, caressed the backs of his thighs, even dared to pinch one of his buttocks, which caused his member to jerk. "I'm going to come."

She squeezed his stones as she pulled off his shaft with a slight pop. "Then do it. I want all of you," she whispered and then sucked on the head of his member, swirling her tongue around that sensitive flesh.

And he nearly fell over the edge. "How did I find a vixen at a rout, and one who is the older sister of my best friend?" His hands on her head tightened, guiding her, holding her steady as he went in and out of her mouth. Seconds later, his eyes rolled back into his head.

I can't last.

It was the closest to heaven he'd ever been. Even now, his length twitched and jerked from her handling. Pre-ejaculate seeped from his tip, and she licked it away. Diana eased her fingers beneath his stones to massage the thin skin directly behind them.

"Fuck!" The word was propelled from his throat with such force and surprise, that she giggled around him. He bucked his hips, sending his shaft deep, while his fingers curled into her hair. "You are going to kill me." The statement was graveled, his body taut as he fought against breaking.

"Let me see you in your basest form." She continued her relentless quest to apparently leave him useless and insane. Again and again, she twisted her fingers about his length while sucking and then soothing with her tongue, followed by taking him deeper into her mouth while he continued to thrust like a man possessed. Every few seconds, she would massage that highly sensitive skin behind his stones.

"Shit, shit, *shit!*" The muscles of his thighs tensed while his grip on her head did the same. "Diana, ah…!"

That was the moment when Nathaniel lost control. With a muffled shout, he hit release. When he tried to pull out, she held him by his arse cheeks, keeping him steady. As he exploded in a powerful release, she swallowed a few times in succession, apparently determined to drain him.

Oddly, in that moment, *something* was shared between them, a bond of sorts, and it was as powerful as the act she'd just finished upon him.

Once he finished spending, he pulled out of her mouth, stepped away from her with shock filling his chest. His breath shuddered from his lungs, ragged and rapid in the silence.

"Damnation," he whispered as he drew her to her feet. "That was… unexpected. Thank you." Genuine honesty echoed in his tone. It had been more than a carnal act. In a way, it felt… sacred if that was possible.

A chuckle escaped her as she wiped at the lingering moisture on her cheeks and lips, even more so when he gave her his handkerchief. "I'm glad you enjoyed it so much, but that was what I felt yesterday. Truly extraordinary."

"Agreed." What was more, he would never be the same again. He stared at her as if he'd never seen her before. Perhaps he hadn't. Who knew she'd hidden such power behind her guise of a widow?

Her eyes sparkled with amusement. "Was it better than what that other woman gave you the other night?"

Yes, she was definitely a minx, and he adored it. "God, yes." He stuffed himself back into his breeches, he couldn't help his grin. In fact, he felt as if he could fly to the moon. "So, what now? What exactly is between us? Do you want an affair?"

"Perhaps I do. An affair full of pleasure and poetry." Then one of her eyebrows rose. "However, what would it entail?"

It sounded far too good to be true, but he yearned for whatever it would be. Finished with the buttons at his front falls, he shot her what felt like a cheeky look. "Come to the Fentons' ball with me tomorrow night and we'll find out together."

Slowly, she nodded. "I'll arrive separately in the event I wish to leave early."

"And it will allow you a certain amount of freedom." He didn't mind, and he respected her for it. "I should probably escort you back. William said you are taking dinner with him and your family this evening." Yet he didn't want to quit her company so soon.

She tucked his handkerchief in her reticule. "I am, to discuss Papa's condition, so it's good I have something to look forward to with you." Then she retrieved her bonnet. When she fit it to her head, he batted her hands away.

"Let me." It was an intimate act, this tying the bow beneath her chin, and he rather liked it. When he met her dark sapphire gaze that brimmed with desperate need, he nearly came undone for a second time, which would have been impossible. "At least we can enjoy a leisurely stroll back to where we left the carriage." As soon as he could, he intended to claim her body, for nothing else would do now.

What the devil is wrong with me?

CHAPTER SIX

April 28, 1817
Fenton House
St. James's Place
Mayfair, London

D IANA GLANCED WITH longing at the double French-paned doors of the ballroom that opened into the back garden of the large townhouse. It was one of the rare properties in St. James's that wasn't attached to its neighbors, and since it stood alone, it was a bit more private than the other homes in the same area.

Yet because it was raining outside, that meant she couldn't make scandalous use of the spring gardens tonight… and she very much wanted a coupling with Lord Holdcraft. After being teased and providing the same to him, she suffered from unfilled longing with desire circling hungrily through her lower belly.

What am I becoming? She feared the answer, for it might not be entirely proper.

The ballroom was crowded and the dance floor even more so with happy, chattering people. Buzzing conversation was punctuated by laughter and greetings. Every once in a while, she saw someone she recognized, and she would either lift a hand or stop by to chat for a few moments. And it was different this time around from when she was married to Atterbury. There was an excitement to each footstep and happiness bubbling through her chest knowing she wouldn't return home to a house where her husband resided, and there was no need to do the pretty with him while in public.

Truth to tell, there was something freeing about being back in society on her own terms, and quite frankly, she reveled in it.

With every step as she made her way around the perimeter of the ballroom, she breathed in the scent of the hothouse flowers in several arrangements placed strategically about the room. Potted ferns and other plants added much needed freshness and a green hue amidst the bouquet of colorful gowns.

Over the next hour, Diana danced sets with a few men, and she hadn't remembered how lovely of a time taking in such exercise was. She flirted with men she found attractive, received compliments on her gown of periwinkle silk, and more than once she let her gloved fingers trace the round amethysts stones in her necklace. Yes, it was delightful to again be in society and wear pretty things for the mere purpose of having people notice her.

As she sipped from a glass of punch one of her admirers had brought for her, Diana could help but wonder where Nathaniel had gotten off to? Was he even now trysting with a younger, prettier lady? After all, he'd made no secret of the fact that he was a rake and that he enjoyed being such. The thought sent a wave of hot irritation through her chest. If that were the case, had what they'd already shared together meant nothing?

By the time she drained her cut-crystal punch glass, she glanced over, and there was the viscount, prowling toward her as if there was no one else in the room than her. Odd flutters went through her lower belly, and her fingers tightened on the glass. There was a certain gleam in his mossy eyes that promised wicked, delicious things if she dared enough to ask him for them.

Did she?

While her heartbeat accelerated, Diana kept her gaze on him. He was so wonderfully handsome in his black evening attire, but it was the sky-blue satin waistcoat that drew her attention to his flat abdomen. As he came closer, she discerned white stars and a silver crescent moon embroidered on the garment.

"Ah, Lord Holdcraft. How lovely to see you here tonight." For the life of her, she couldn't remember the words to anything more erudite than that.

What is wrong with me? I'm not an untried young woman at her first ball!

"Equally as lovely as seeing you, Lady Diana." A mysterious grin curved his lips, and all she wanted to do was curl her fingers into his cravat, pull him to her, and then kiss him for as long as she liked. "I must say, it appears that you've become quite popular. You have not lacked partners tonight."

How long had he been watching her? With a frown, she set her empty glass onto a silver tray of a passing footman before giving the viscount the whole of her attention. "Never say that annoys you. I'm as surprised at my success as you. Only this time, I've much more experience and wisdom behind me."

"Perhaps you should use a tad more discernment. At least one of the men you danced with tonight is a bounder with pockets to let. I don't wish for you to be taken advantage of," he said as he drew her along the wall until they stood near the doors that led into the corridor and away from where a group of wallflowers sat in delicate chairs with gilt legs.

"I don't believe I asked for your protection," Diana replied with a hint of frost in her voice. "And all I did was dance. There was no contract offered and no promises made."

He grunted. "I can do no less than look out for you since you are my best friend's sister."

"Ha." A trace of amusement went through her chest. She refused to let him off that easily, so she crossed her arms beneath her breast, and lifted an eyebrow when the viscount's gaze briefly dipped to her décolletage. "Why is it acceptable for men to draw women to them for anything from flirting to trysting, but when a woman does the same, those same men turn angry and possessive?" To be fair, it was fun to tease him, and the fact he did show a bit of possession only deepened the interest surrounding him.

"I'm not either one of those things."

"Are you certain?" When he didn't answer, she pressed her advantage with a faint smile. "Then you must be jealous? Otherwise, you wouldn't have said anything." Was that true, then? "And if that is the crux of your grumpiness tonight, you need to have a good look at yourself." She lowered her voice to a barely audible whisper. "Just because you and I had a bit of fun together, that doesn't give you the right to restrict whatever I wish to do in my own life. Especially since you aren't willing to give up the lifestyle you've chosen for yourself."

Shock went through his expression, and his eyes widened, but the dratted man grinned. "Touche. Perhaps I *am* jealous."

"Oh? I'm surprised that you admitted it." This whole conversation was delightful.

A dark flush rose over his cravat on his neck. "Not much else I can do. How you managed to call me out on it is the true question of the night, though."

Diana shrugged. "Someone needs to do so. You seem to need to be taken firmly in hand and shown another way of living."

The wicked expression returned, and he dropped his voice as he shuffled a bit closer. "Is that what you've planned, then? To take me firmly in hand? For that sounds quite delightful."

Heat sprang into her cheeks, and though she wanted to narrow her gaze at him for stepping over the line, she couldn't, for she wished to do exactly that to him; he was just a stop along the journey of her soul's freedom.

Wasn't he?

"That depends on what happens from this point forward tonight."

"Ah." Slowly, he nodded. "How many of the men you've danced with tonight did you agree to have call on you later this week?"

The poor thing couldn't help himself. Diana's smile widened. The feeling of womanly power that rose in her chest was rather interesting, for she'd never had that before. "If you must know, I didn't ask any of them to call. They were perfectly lovely to share a dance with, but they are all too immature to want them hanging about my life, even at the periphery."

It was adorable how the viscount's expression lightened at her answer. "I see." He drew her closer to the door but paused before escaping the room. "I wouldn't blame you if you wished to take one of the young pups to bed and show him a thing or two."

"Do stop, Holdcraft." She gently rapped the spine of her closed fan on his chest. "I am certainly not *that* sort of widow." Unless it involved the man standing before her right this minute. Yet as they continued to talk, there was no shortage of female eyes that followed Nathaniel's progress through the room or shot her daggers that she'd been able to snag his attention. Was she merely making a fool of herself for tarrying with him at all? Perhaps she should step aside and the let the younger women have a turn. Too bad she was quite stubborn. "At this stage of my life, I *do* enjoy more intelligent conversations than how much a man likes to hunt or what is going on in parliament."

Then the string quintet struck the opening notes of a waltz. Couples proceeded to fill empty spots on the parquet dance floor. It reminded her of happy colors within a spring floral bouquet seeing all those skirts and waistcoats beneath the candlelight.

Nathaniel softly cleared his throat. "Would you like to dance this set or the next with me, Lady Diana?" He waggled his red eyebrows. "I'll wager I'm a better partner than the ones you've already partnered tonight."

"No thank you. I don't feel like dancing any more tonight."

"Oh." His expression fell, and a trace of disappointment went through his eyes, much to her continued amusement. "What do you want to do with the remainder of the night?"

"Honestly?" When he nodded, she continued. "I really just want to talk. With you," she said with what she hoped was a speaking glance. "I would like to know you better, listen to the things you care about in life."

"I see." Hope sprang into his face, and it was as if the sun came out from behind the clouds. "Then by all means, let us remove to a more quiet room, especially since your brother told me he would also be in attendance at this ball."

She frowned. "William is here?" With a glance look about the ballroom, she huffed. Her heartbeat accelerated, for he would come the crab if he caught her going out of the room with his best friend. No doubt Nathaniel's reputation made her brother feel overly protective in regard to her. "He didn't inform me of his plans, and I haven't seen him yet tonight."

"The last time I spoke with him, he expressed an avid interest in attending. Of course, he could have changed his mind depending on his whim or what your parents wish."

"That is true. I'm afraid he won't take Papa's death well." To be fair, neither would she, but William wasn't as experienced in death. "It will be quite the sorrowful time."

"Well, since I'm his best friend, I will be there supporting him. Not to mention what you and I have done together this week warrants at least me helping you through the loss." He cleared his throat again. "That is, if you wish it."

Before she could respond, a man perhaps ten years her junior came up to them both. When he murmured an apology, he then turned the whole of his attention on Diana.

"I would enjoy it above all things if you would promise me a dance tonight, my lady," he said in a deep whisper that ordinarily would have pleased her, but at the present time, she simply wasn't interested a man so much younger than herself.

I already have my hands full with Holdcraft, and I'm not nearly done with him.

"Unfortunately, I—"

That was when Nathaniel forcefully put space between her and the newcomer. "Off you go, Mr. Aldren. The lady is spoken for the rest of the evening. You'll need to go bedevil some other lady tonight."

The younger man bristled. While the candlelight made his blond hair glimmer, he dared to ignore the viscount and instead took up one of her hands. "I won't go unless Lady Diana gives me that directive."

"Truly, Mr. Aldren, while I appreciate your interest, I'm afraid Lord Holdcraft is correct. I have other commitments for the remainder of the night." And if fate were kind, they would involve the viscount's naked body being wrapped around hers.

What has gotten into me since meeting him?

"You heard her, Aldren. Off you pop," Nathaniel said with what could only be described as unholy glee in his expression.

Ruddy color crawled up the younger man's neck. "Perhaps another time, then," he said in a rather stilted voice. Then, with a nod, he moved away from them toward the gaggle of wallflowers at the far end of the room.

Diana bit the inside of her cheek to keep from laughing. "That wasn't well done of you. There was no call to be rude."

"Perhaps, but it was definitely needed." When he smirked, she snorted with laughter.

Good heavens, when was the last time she'd had so much fun at a society event? Or with a man, for that matter? "Rogue."

"I did warn you." He gestured at the doorway with his chin. "Shall we? If you would rather I scout out a spot in the house, I can manage that as well. You could join me later."

That sounded far too complicated, and she simply didn't have the wherewithal for it. "Why don't we remove to the entry hall? Guests are milling about everywhere else, and I suspect our host and hostess invited far too many people than the house can hold."

"One of the pitfalls of wishing to make a sensation." Seconds later, the viscount left the ballroom, and then she followed.

Honestly, she didn't much care if gossips wished to attach rumor to her name. It wasn't as if she were making her debut in society, and after surviving her marriage, perhaps it was time to shake a few things up a bit.

By the time they arrived in the lavish entry hall where oil paintings of landscapes decorated the walls in gilt frames, there was only a footman hanging about, no doubt ready and waiting to fetch wraps and hats should guests wish to leave early. She and Nathaniel both ignored him.

"Come, sit beside me," she asked in a low voice as she settled onto a settee with a gilt-painted frame. The cushions were of crushed golden velvet. When he did, she asked, "You have mentioned a few times that you are a rake and a rogue. I wish to know if you have ever fallen in love?"

"I have." He nodded as he rested his gloved hands on his knees. "Twice. Once as a young man of twenty. I'd foolishly fallen for an heiress who I thought held the same feelings as me. Unfortunately, she only wanted me for what I could do for her carnally."

"Ah, so was that when you embarked on a life of shallow liaisons? So you wouldn't have your heart broken again?" It was an interesting look into his life.

"I suppose it was, now that you mention it." Surprise lay stamped across his face. "I'd never entertained the idea before." For the space of a few heartbeats, he remained silent before speaking again. "The second time came a handful of years later. I'd fallen hard and fast. In fact, I was on the verge of asking for her hand."

"What happened?" Despite herself, Diana was swept away on the story.

He shrugged. "Two weeks later, she announced that she was engaged to a different man, one who had a much higher title than I did, and one who was wealthy beyond her wildest dreams." A huff of annoyance escaped him. "Apparently, she desired that much more than she did genuine love."

"Which made you shun the very idea of marriage altogether." The bits and pieces of his life were coming together into the puzzle she knew him to be now.

"Perhaps. I suppose I'm a bit broken in that way."

"Or else you simply need to let yourself try again. The next woman to hold your heart might prove to break your unlucky streak." Odd, but the thought of him with another woman caused her chest to tighten and a wave of irrational anger sweep over her.

"Said woman would need to prove herself much different than the others."

Diana nodded. "Have you done anything over the course of your life that will prove as your legacy? Meaning have you involved yourself into charities or causes that don't directly benefit you?"

"Beyond wanting to dabble in poetry?" His slightly crooked grin sent frissons of need twisting down her spine. "I fund a few causes throughout London. One for widows, one for the care of orphans, and one to provide day-old loaves of bread to the less fortunate in areas such as the Dials."

Surprise moved through her. "That's wonderful, and a bit surprising." One wouldn't think that a rake like him would think along those lines.

"About five years ago, I had a riding accident that brought to me a crossroads. I realized that my life was more than a bit shallow and wasteful, so I wished to change that." A sigh escaped him. "It helps to balance being a rake. Or, at least I hope it does."

"I rather think it will, when all is said and done." Her respect and admiration for him went up a notch. Too bad they weren't alone. She wanted to kiss him, see him naked, bite his skin, explore his body at her leisure.

When he touched a hand to her arm, he grinned and lowered his voice. "Shutter your eyes, Diana."

"Why?"

"Because we will land in scandal if you don't." Yet the look in *his* eyes suggested he wouldn't mind that at all.

She snorted. "I doubt that. I'm a widow and you're a known rake." Not that any of those things made a difference. The dragons of society could mind their own business.

"Regardless, there is heat in your eyes that suggests you'll throw me up against the nearest wall and do wicked things to me in a few moments."

A shiver of need ripped down her spine to lodge deep in her core. "What if I want to do exactly that?" The man beside her was having a scandalous effect on her. How was that possible?

A dark flush rushed up his neck, and it was as adorable as everything else she'd discovered about him.

After a chuckle, she asked, "What? You didn't expect such an appetite from a woman older than you?"

"To be honest, I didn't. Silly of me, surely, for women of all ages can become aroused and participate in carnal games, and I find that quite interesting from you."

She allowed herself a small smile. "If we're fortunate. Growing older as a woman isn't kind, and there are times when I don't feel quite the thing, but those urges are still there. I still have needs, but some of them come with the hope of merely being held until whatever storm I'm fighting with manages to pass."

Was it embarrassing to admit that to him? Perhaps a bit, but it was the truth.

"A man would be a nodcock not to want to embrace everything you represent." For long moments, he held her gaze then dared to take one of her hands and squeeze her fingers. "In light of what you've said, perhaps it's time for us to remove from such a stifling place."

"Ha. You're learning, Holdcraft." A chuckle followed her statement.

Twenty minutes later, he assisted her into his closed carriage, and the rain hadn't let up since earlier in the evening. Before he joined her, he asked, "Do you wish to go home?"

"I do not." Heat enveloped her, for she intended to act quite brazen tonight.

"Very well." Nathaniel nodded. To his driver, he said, "To my townhouse."

"Of course, Lord Holdcraft," the man said as the viscount joined her in the carriage.

Once he'd closed the door and the vehicle lurched into motion, Diana sat beside him on his bench. This addition to the night would be much more fun than the ball.

"It's lovely how well you follow instructions, Nathaniel." Then she pulled him close by his cravat. "That bodes well for other things, don't you think?"

A growl came from his throat as his arms went around her. "I do indeed." Seconds later, he claimed her lips in an intense kiss that set her blood aflame.

Excitement buzzed through her, and she gave herself up to his ministrations. Heavens help her, but there was no going back now.

CHAPTER SEVEN

No. 10
Bedford Square
Mayfair, London

NATHANIEL WAS MORE than a bit smug as he ushered Diana up the short walkway to the blue-painted door to his townhouse.

After all, why shouldn't he take her to his home? She hadn't specified where she wanted to go after they'd left the ball, and after the blatant looks and flirting they'd exchanged while in the ballroom, there was only one way that he wanted the night to end.

Never had he desired a woman more than he did Diana in this moment.

As he led her into the library on the main floor, the longcase clock on the level above struck the eleventh hour of the night. Though it was dark—for his staff probably didn't expect him back until the wee hours of the morning—he knew the layout of the room like the proverbial back of his hand.

"Would you care for refreshments?" While waiting for her response, Nathaniel lit a few candles about the space. Not enough illumination to read but enough to cast weird shadows over the ceiling and leave mysterious pockets of darkness in the corners.

"I wouldn't say no to some tea, that is if your staff is still awake. If not, I can either make it myself or do without."

Every new side to her that he uncovered was fascinating. "My butler will be awake reading. He usually is up until I return home from society events." As he spoke, he moved across the room then gave the brocade bellpull a tug. "Feel free to settle in or peruse the shelves. I'll join you in a moment." A few moments later, the butler answered the summons, and once Nathaniel ordered the tea, he then went over to the shelf that she inspected near one of the candles.

"From what I can see of your collection, it's impressive."

"Thank you. I've worked hard on finding each and every book." After that brief bout of kissing in the carriage, he was acutely aware of her. The heat of her, the scent of her called him to her, and it took all his willpower not to take her into his arms. "I still need more books of poetry, and there are a few volumes from Shakespeare that I'm missing."

"Books are such cozy and exciting companions." She slipped her fingertips along the spines. "I'm so grateful to have had the privilege of learning how to read, of having books in my possession, of spending time with them."

Before he could respond, the butler returned with a silver tea service on a matching tray.

"Thank you, Waterson. It's much appreciated."

The man on the shorter side with graying blond hair nodded as he set the tray on the low table in the center of the room. "It is no trouble, my lord. We are just beginning to put the house to bed."

Nathaniel nodded while Diana continued to look through the bookshelves. He removed his gloves and tossed them onto a small rose-inlaid occasional table nearby. "That should be all we require for the remainder of the night, so please, go ahead and retire. I will escort Lady Diana home after we are finished here." Whether that be only the tea or other, more strenuous endeavors after that.

"Of course, my lord." With a curious glance in Diana's direction, the butler departed, then Nathaniel softly closed the door behind him.

"How do you take your tea?" he asked his guest, even though doing something as mundane that taking in the refreshing beverage and cakes was the last thing he wished to do in this moment.

"Oh, with a splash of cream and a small lump of sugar, especially if taking it in the afternoon." She flashed him a smile as she came toward the grouping of furniture where he sat on a low sofa. "If I'm drinking it the first thing in the morning, I don't have anything in it to dilute the strength." The moment she sat in a chair near his location, she took off her gloves and laid them on the tabletop.

"Why is that?"

She shrugged. "There are times when I have trouble waking. I just want to burrow into my bedding and sleep for another few hours, but there are duties to attend."

"That's adorable." As he busied himself with fixing her tea, he looked at her. "You are free to do whatever you wish, so spend your time however you like. There are no demands on you, and I'd say you've earned it after everything."

"Thank you for that. Perhaps one of these days I will, but I always feel as if I'm wasting my day if I lounge about. While the rest of the *ton* is laying abed, I'm usually up and making inroads into the things on my daily diary." When she accepted the delicate china teacup from him, their fingers brushed. Awareness raced over his skin from the contact.

"Your life has been much different than my own that I'm in awe of all you've done." He stirred a lump of sugar into his tea.

"Do stop, Holdcraft. I have merely been a wife and a mother, and more recently, a patron of various arts throughout London." Yet the blush in her cheeks betrayed her pleasure at his praise. "Speaking of which, if you and I spend more time together, I will ask that you read your favorite poetry to me. I adore hearing such lines aloud."

That smacked far too much of domestication, and for one

moment, panic moved through his chest, but then he shoved the thought from his mind. "I would be honored, but to read you the poetry of your choice as well as to have you with me for far longer than tonight."

Did that mean they were ready, indeed, to embark upon the affair?

She drew the tip of her tongue along her bottom lip, presumably to catch a drop of tea… or to tease him. It didn't matter, for interest went through his shaft, rapidly hardening it. "What are you planning to do with me tonight, Nathaniel? You and I are both past the age of being coy or playing at seduction."

"Why, my lady, are you accusing me of having designs on you?" He couldn't help but teasing her as he sipped his tea.

"Is that how you took my comment?" One of her eyebrows rose in challenge.

"Mmm." He shrugged. "Though, you must admit there are some advantages to a seduction."

"True." This time she winked, and need pulsed through his length. Wanting a distraction until he could be certain most of his staff had indeed either left for their own homes or had sought out their beds, he said, "Tell me about your children."

"Well, Percy is twenty, and he's successfully taken the Atterbury title. I expect him in London soon." As she spoke about her son, her features softened and maternal love shone in her eyes. "He is growing out of that awkward young man stage and into a handsome adult."

"Does he take after you?"

"In some ways. He has my curls and his hair is also light brown like mine." Pausing to sip her tea, she watched him in the dim illumination. "But there is more than a little of his father in him. I only hope he continues to mature into a man who is nothing like Atterbury."

"There is no doubt in my mind that he will, since you have had a hand in raising him." Nathaniel nodded. "And you will show him how to respect women, of that I have no doubt."

"I hope you're right." After draining her cup, Diana set it into the saucer then rested them both on the table in front of her. "I'm looking forward to seeing what he'll do for the title and how he'll bring respectability to it again." She remained silent for a bit before speaking again. "As for Eliza, well, she is going to be quite independent, I think. Quite headstrong at seventeen already."

"And why should she not? Her mother is quite a lovely role model for that."

Another faint blush went through her cheeks. "I don't know about that, but just now, she is away at a finishing school in Brighton. However, she'll come to London with my son, who will fetch her before he arrives into Town. Any day, I imagine."

The obvious love she had for her children was both endearing and daunting. Did he fit into her life being the sort of man that he was? "You will probably be happy to see them again."

"I will, of course, though I wish the reunion was for a happier reason." When the happiness from seconds before faded beneath sorrow, he immediately wanted to bring her back to that elevated place.

"What do you want from your future, Diana?" After putting his cup and saucer onto the table, he left the sofa long enough to slide over the sofa toward her chair.

"After having the life I already did, this time around, I wish to chase happiness on my terms. Will that mean marriage? That largely depends on the man, and since I'm well beyond the age that pregnancy is possible, I feel I have more freedom than I did as a young woman."

Interesting. "Whatever you decide will prove amazing, I'll wager, merely because that is the sort of woman you are." Damn, but he was going heavy-handed with the compliments this evening. Would it make him seem desperate?

"I appreciate that." Hunger and desire had returned to her deep sapphire gaze. "How do you wish for your future to look?"

"I haven't thought about it for a while, but I want to be ful-filled, and oddly enough, like you, I do want happiness, perhaps security. All of that sounds so foreign to me while that this place in my life, but for the past few months or so, playing at being the rake has paled as time goes on."

"Then you want something more permanent?" Was that hope in her voice?

"I might, depending on the woman and if other things come to fruition." Over the years, he'd made certain his estate turned a profit and with clever investments, he had a decent annual income to support a wife and a possible family.

Yet he'd barely agreed to an affair with *this* woman. Shouldn't he set aside time to explore that first?

"It's a good decision, moving away from your rakish image. And who knows? You might find something else you are wildly talented at." As she spoke, Diana left her chair and stepped over to where he perched on the sofa. "However, right now, there *is* one thing I want from you."

"Oh?" He could hardly think because his pulse pounded so loudly in his head.

"Yes, and I've thought of nothing else for the past day or so." She drew him to his feet with a gentle tug to his cravat. "I want you to thoroughly put me through my paces."

"Why?" It was damned arousing to be with a woman who knew exactly what she wanted.

"I never had that during my marriage, and it's quite dull setting myself off by my fingers when I want a release."

If he wasn't careful, he'd spend in his pants by her words alone, but he kept tight control over himself. Needing something to do with his hands, he held her head between his palms and stared into her eyes. "Is that your permission? You want *everything* done to you tonight?"

She nodded. "It is."

Excitement buzzed at the base of his spine while acute need enveloped his stones. "Shall I undress you, then?"

"I…" Need warred with panic in her eyes. Why was she so nervous? She had been married, had enjoyed physical relations with her husband—shoddy as they'd been—had borne children! Perhaps she was feeling unsure, much like an innocent, since this was practically new to her after what she'd already shared with him. "I think so, yes, and I'm acting the ninny, aren't I?"

"You are not. It's perfectly understandable. After twenty-two years with a man who couldn't stumble his way around a woman's body, you don't want that to happen again."

"Yes." Diana nodded. "But I know you won't be that."

"I will not, and haven't I already sent you flying?" As he spoke, he removed his tailcoat, tossed it away, and then divested himself of the waistcoat, where it joined the jacket on the floor nearby.

"You have, and it was spectacular." Her darkened gaze glittered as his cuffs, collar, and cravat came off to follow the other garments to the carpet.

"Come here." Before she could do anything else, Nathaniel settled on the sofa once more with his legs outstretched. "Sit between my legs." When she did so, his legs framed hers and her wrapped his arms around her. The hardness of his erection bumped insistently against her arse. "I'll wager your husband never did anything like this." He pressed his lips to the side of her neck, and enjoyed the faint floral scent of her skin.

"He would rather die than have relations anywhere except a bed." By increments, she relaxed against him.

"I hope you know he was an idiot." The more he nibbled the skin beneath her ear, the longer he drew a hand up and down her arm, the more tiny shivers ran through her to transfer to him.

"Oh, I do. Even more so than you do."

Nathaniel snorted. "Shall I continue?"

"God, yes."

"Good." He licked and kissed a path along the side of her neck. All the while, he continued to stroke a hand up and down her arm. When she fidgeted, he brushed the fingers of his other hand along the top of her bodice. "If you feel uncomfortable, bid me nay and I'll immediately stop."

"At the moment, I want to feel your hands on me."

The woman was incredible. "Fair enough." When he dipped a finger beneath her gown to briefly graze a hardened nipple, she sucked in a breath.

"I can hardly breathe, yet you've barely started." She reached up a hand and hooked her fingers about his nape, gently pulling his head closer.

"It's good that we're compatible in this way then, hmm?"

"Quite." When she turned her head, he captured her lips with his, and for several minutes, they spoke with kisses and fleeting caresses.

Eventually, and he was never quite certain how it had happened, he managed to divest Diana of her clothing. Only then did he shuck out of his evening breeches, hosiery, and shoes. Once they were both nude, he settled her once more between his legs. In the dim candlelight, her skin was pale yet pink, and she was the most gorgeous woman.

"I knew you would be beautiful," he whispered against her neck, and ever so gently he drew his fingers along her sides, played her ribs as if he were a pianist.

"Gammon." Her eyes fluttered closed, and she reclined into him, both relaxed yet alert. "Childbirth and surviving Atterbury has given me more curves than are fashionable."

"You merely need to see them in a different light." Nathaniel cupped her breasts, and she sucked in a breath. "You are lovely, lush, and I cannot wait to explore."

"Such a charmer. No wonder every woman in London fancies herself in love with you." Diana sighed when he squeezed her breasts, rolled those dark pink nipples at the roots. "Oh, yes, do that."

"Like that, do you?" His lips glanced against the side of her neck as he spoke. The fact she'd allowed him such intimate access wasn't lost on him.

God, William will kill me if he finds out.

"I'm nearly gone, and you've only played with my breasts."

"Good. You deserve everything I'll give and more." When he glanced his palms over her erect nipples, a shuddering moan escaped her. She arched her back, which put her firmly into his care.

Honestly, he couldn't have enough.

"I need so much more, Nathaniel." Then she wriggled her bottom, and when he groaned from the sensations streaking through his shaft, she laughed. "Please."

Bloody hell, but she felt simply amazing in his arms, and the tiny plea she uttered set fire to his veins. He couldn't help thinking he was the most fortunate of men to have gained this extraordinary woman's trust. Best friend be damned, he couldn't wait to claim her body and begin their affair.

The thoughts humbled him as he caressed the perfect globes of her breasts. With each pass of his hands, each stroke and twist of his fingers on those pert nipples, she moaned and arched her back. Clearly it had been years since she'd been pleasured by a man who knew what he was doing, and if she was this wanting, it wouldn't take long for her to fall over the edge into bliss.

As he slipped a hand down her torso, past the soft swell of her belly, over her mons to delve his fingers into the curls shrouding her sex, the soft sounds of pleasure and encouragement she made went straight to his shaft. It would be only a matter of time before he embarrassed himself by spending too soon, but he gritted his teeth and ignored the throbbing discomfort.

Right now, his focus was on Diana, in caring for her needs, in showing her that she had always been deserving of carnal pleasure, even if her husband couldn't see it.

The dear woman parted her legs to allow him greater access, and as he spread her folds to uncover the swelling pearl at her center, she whimpered. She held his other hand to her breast, pressing it to the nipple. "Make me fly," she whispered.

How could he ignore that? At the first pass of his fingers, she moaned. The shiver that went through her delicious body transferred to him. By the second, she was shaking with need.

Nathaniel circled that tiny bundle of nerves, experimented with varying levels of friction as he worked it over, and all the while, he kissed the side of her neck, plucked and rolled her nipple. When her breath came in labored pants, he grinned and whispered words of encouragement into her ear.

"So different from the other day, but so familiar." Her breaths came in pants. "I am overwhelmed."

"Shall I stop?"

"Heavens, no!"

With a chuckle, he worried that swollen bud, rubbed it, circled it as if that were his only purpose in life.

"Mmm, yes." The lady writhed against his body, and his hardened length pulsed with a need of its own. "Dear God, I'm going to be swallowed by these sensations." There was both marvel and worry in her tones.

"Then let them swallow you." Ignoring the urgency in his shaft, he sought to push her toward the brink, and for one second, he left off working her nubbin in favor of slipping two fingers into the honeyed heat of her passage. A ragged moan left his throat, for she was so damned wet and welcoming. Christ, but he couldn't wait to claim her; she was warm and tight, and as he finger-fucked her, that passage pulled at his digits.

"Fly if you wish, Diana." In and out, in and out he thrust into her. "Relax and let yourself go. Once you fall over that edge, there is so much more I'll do to you."

"Merciful heavens…" Her head thrashed on his chest. "Saying it won't make the reality come easier…"

"Shh. It'll come." So would they both. Renewing his attentions at her breast, Nathaniel withdrew from her passage only to bedevil her nubbin with greater intensity. "Tell me what you want me to do to you."

"Just this. I'll do—Oh!" A shiver racked her body, but he didn't let up on the friction, the play he did to her button or her nipple. "Ah!" When she fell into that release, she did it in spectacular fashion. Diana shattered in his arms. A low, keening cry left her throat as her body stiffened, then relaxed. The flicker of expressions on her face tugged at his chest, as did the way she pointed her toes as the orgasm crashed over her, and her eyes shuttered closed. She clutched his arm, tightened and released her fingers on it, while contractions and waves of pleasure no doubt stole through her person.

It was one of the most glorious sights he'd ever seen, and it made him wonder why he couldn't remember the same with any of the other women he'd been with.

But he wasn't done with her. Not by half. As soon as she came back to herself, Nathaniel encouraged her off his lap.

Immediately, she frowned as she stood awkwardly by the sofa. "What are you doing? Have you tired of me already?"

He scoffed as he stood to take her into his arms once more. "Hardly." With a flush of pleasure barely staining her cheeks and chest in the dim illumination, and her hair half escaping its pins, it was almost as if she'd stepped out of a dream to be with him this night. "Dear God, you are incredible. Did you know that?" Putting his hands on either side of her neck, he drew her to him and kissed her, slowly at first because he was in awe of her, and then, once urgent heat roared through him, he deepened the embrace.

There was no going back now.

CHAPTER EIGHT

RESIDUAL TREMORS FLUTTERED through Diana's body as she held the viscount's gaze. "Why are you not seeing to my pleasure, Lord Holdcraft?" Even in this, she couldn't resist teasing him, for he'd already done so much more for her—to her—than her husband had ever done in twenty-two years of marriage.

"My apologies. Let me rectify that post haste," he said with heat and humor in his eyes.

When he reached for her, Diana uttered a soft squeal and darted toward one of the shelves and away from the grouping of furniture. "You'll have to try harder than that." Who knew carnal relations could be so whimsical or fun?

"Ah, is that how it's going to be tonight, then?" With a grin of his own, he stalked her over the floor, chuckling when she retreated. "Why so skittish, my dove?"

The endearment gave her pause, but then she put it out of her mind. "As I said, it's very different from what I've known before." She shook her head, for with that look in his eyes and the way he prowled over the floor sent tingles of need through her lower belly. "You are quite intense." Then she let her gaze rove over his naked body, from the lean length of him, to his slightly ridged abdomen, to his rampantly erect member, he was every inch a rake of some account.

"Well, I'm hardly like Atterbury," he scoffed.

"No, you are not. Thank goodness." And she couldn't wait to play with that thick shaft of his. With a giggle, Diana nodded as he stepped close to her, easily trapping her between his large body and the bookshelf. "I doubt any woman has bid you nay when sexual release is in the offing."

"Perhaps, but there is only one woman I am interested in pleasing tonight." He gently tugged her into his arms, and seconds later claimed her lips with his.

Despite her pinwheeling thoughts, Diana slid a hand up his chest to rest at his shoulder, and slowly, she gave herself into his care. He was the first man to see her naked since her husband and he would be the first man she coupled with since him as well. Did that show flawed logic, or merely carnal desperation, ever since he'd brought her to release with his mouth?

Not knowing, she shoved that thought away as well in favor of kissing him back.

Every nerve in her body felt alive and on edge. The fires in her blood became molten rivers of need, and she gasped at the intensity of desire sparking between them. With a sound that was both a moan and a cry, she looped her arms about his shoulders and clung to him without a shred of decency or decorum as she returned that embrace.

"You are quite the siren," he whispered while taking her more comfortably in his arms and teasing her with intense kisses that hinted at exactly what he wished to do next.

"Such gammon, but I rather like the description. Perhaps I should do this more often with other men. You know, to compare skills." It was far too easy to tease him.

"If you do while we're conducting an affair, I can't be held responsible for all the clocks I'll clean for such trespasses." He moved his hands up her back. "I want you so much, but I alternately wish to make this interlude last."

She snorted. "If we are truly having an affair, that assumes we will do this many more times in the future."

"Good thinking, and yes, we will definitely have more of this."

"Mmm, I can't wait." Then her propriety fled, for she dragged her lips beneath the sharp line of his jaw, licked a path down the strong column of his throat merely to discover if it would drive him wild.

"Diana…" A groan issued from him as he drew his palms up her sides to cup her breasts. "Damn, but having you in my arms, naked and willing…" He shook his head. Seconds later, he nipped and nibbled the side of her neck. "My young man self is stunned by the audacity, yet rejoicing at the luck."

The fact he'd had a crush on her years ago sent a wave of heat through her chest. "Well, let's give that young man something to gawk at, hmm?"

"I rather think this session belongs to no one but you and me as we are now." Nathaniel held her breasts, squeezed them, teased the nipples until she whimpered with anticipation. "Rather desperate, aren't you?" he whispered, when she arched her back.

"Yes, of course I am, especially since you've already made me fall over the edge once tonight," she said on the heels of a gasp while he continued to bedevil her breasts. When he stimulated her nipples, intense sensations streaked from her breasts to her core. "Please touch me, Nathaniel." If that made her a wanton, then so be it. Never in the whole of her marriage had she implored Atterbury for anything.

"Mmm, begging. I could get used to that," he murmured and gave her nipples a quick pinch. When a sound that was a mix of a gasp and a moan escaped her, he chuckled. "I would love to hear you do more of that for many other things we have no time for, right now."

"Something to look forward to, hmm?" she asked as she stared up into his face. "One of the rewards of having an affair?" Suddenly, she couldn't wait to start.

Humor twinkled in his mossy eyes. "Absolutely."

"It will mean you'll need to give up all other women if you wish to have me."

"I consider that more than a fair trade."

"Cheeky." Was he being truthful or saying that for her benefit? Did it matter in this moment? Diana's head lolled onto her shoulder, for his attentions were quite potent. "Nathaniel…" A shiver racked her being while he continued to manipulate those aching buds.

"I know." Quickly, he urged her arms above her head then caught her wrists in one hand and cupped a breast with the other as her back was pressed against the shelf of books. He nibbled a path along the column of her throat, licked and nipped her breasts, teased her with his hot breath on her skin. "There is so much I wish to do merely to see your reaction, hear the sounds you'll make as I send you to the brink."

"Haven't you already witnessed that tonight, as well as the first time you dared to touch me?"

"Yes, but there is so much more."

"We have plenty of time." She expelled a soft moan when he bedeviled her nipple with his tongue and teeth. "Please! I need you inside me."

"Not just yet, I think, unless you can convince me quite handily." With a wink, he released her wrists and then spread his arms wide. "Would you care to try?"

"Don't be an arse, Holdcraft." If she sounded more waspish than she should, it was because she didn't like being denied, but she caught his head between her hands, pushed up onto her toes, and then kissed him as if she didn't have any shame. Perhaps she didn't, and that didn't matter either. Already she would melt into a puddle at his feet if he didn't hurry. When it didn't appear he was on the same level of desperation as her, Diana slipped a hand between them to cup his equipage, gave him a good squeeze and a bit of a fondle. Oh, she wanted time to explore his bits. "I want you."

"Damn it, woman. I'll spend if you don't leave off." Desperation propelled the words from his throat, but he grinned as he pulled away.

One of her eyebrows rose in challenge. "Really? You cave

after just one touch?"

"I'm nearly insane with desire for you. But there will be retribution for that."

"So many promises, and from a rake, no less. Will you keep them, I wonder?"

"Do you doubt me?" Confusion briefly flickered in his eyes.

"Should I?" Not giving him a chance to answer, with a last caress to his hot, hard shaft, she once more put her hands on his shoulders. "Don't waste time. I want you to claim me, show me why you're so sought after within society for just this purpose."

With an intensity that stole her ability to speak, Nathaniel pinned her between his hard chest and the shelf. She felt the individual book spines against her skin, and it was quite a lovely sensation. The kisses he treated her to were deep and drugging; he dueled with her tongue as they both fought through the flames in their blood and the clouds of desire to find common ground.

When he encouraged one of her legs upward, she hooked it over his hip and wrapped her arms about his strong, broad shoulders. In this moment, in his embrace, there was an odd mix of security, contentment, and desire pressing upon her that hadn't been present within her marriage. Interesting that it came from this man. His eyes were dark with need, and his hands were at her buttocks holding her against the shelf as he set out to apparently devour her whole. Diana forgot everything as she wriggled into a better position, clung to him while she kissed him back. She shuddered as he fit his tip to her opening. Her moan of satisfaction sounded overly loud to her ears, but he swallowed the remainder of the noise and at the same time, he flexed his hips, penetrated her swift and deep, to the hilt without stopping.

And it was like being given a gift she'd no idea was coming.

"Merciful heavens." Awe threaded through her utterance, for this was every bit as satisfying as she'd hoped, and frankly, the worry of being discovered enhanced the act. The viscount was large, thick, and he filled her so completely she wanted to cry from the perfection of that joining. But her eyes shuttered closed as she savored the coupling, while the most delicious sensations bounced through her insides. "Though I'm enjoying the hell out of this, I'm also angry that I was cheated of it for so many years."

"Then you have much to look forward to." He moved, thrusting with short strokes, forcefully spearing into her, which set her blood on fire and each nerve ending tingling.

As best as she could, Diana matched his rhythm. Nathaniel continued to move, so she pulled him closer with her leg around his waist.

Over and over, he drove like a man possessed. Books tumbled from the shelf to fall onto the floor with dull thuds and fluttering pages. She held him to her, kissed whatever portion of his body she encountered. The scrape of her nipples against the coarse sprinkling of red hair on his chest added another layer of heightened sensation to their actions, as did the friction put on the button at the center of her pleasure, for her body was opened to him.

"Oh, dear God," she managed to whisper between pants.

"I've never been called that before," he joked, with a strained chuckle.

The frantic rawness of the act bent all her misconceptions of coitus she'd had while with Atterbury, and she couldn't help but respond in kind as a wild, abandoned woman. "For the first time in my life, I've given myself the freedom to chase my own satisfaction. I'm finally enjoying intercourse."

"You should have been well loved by your husband. I'm sorry you weren't." One of his thrusts went particularly deep then. "Enjoy everything about this fuck, Diana, for there is more to come."

"I… Oh!" Did it make her a horrible person to look forward to being thoroughly pleasured by this man multiple times in the coming months? Then she gave herself up to his advances. His ragged breathing echoed in her ears and his fingers dug into her hips with a savageness that would no doubt leave bruises. Sweat dampened his forehead, his upper lip, and as she kissed him, the taste of salt came away on her tongue.

Frankly, it was damned arousing.

When he delved a hand between their bodies and he strummed his fingers over that swollen bud at her center, she sucked in a breath, and release would hopefully come quickly. Before the scream could leave her throat, he kissed her again, took the sound into himself. Quite simply, they shared a few breaths as their bodies worked to become one. All too soon, the pressure building and circling in her lower belly broke, for the sensory overload had finally overwhelmed her.

"Oh… ah!" The half-muffled utterance sounded overly loud in the silence of the room. Contractions fluttered through her core as pleasure swamped her in ever-increasing waves. Diana dug her fingers into his shoulders, hoping to leave *her* mark on *him*. She whispered his name as if in prayer, buried her face in the crook of his shoulder, and still the bands of release kept coming. There was no relenting, no cessation, and she marveled over that fact.

Another two thrusts sent him into the vortex with her. The viscount claimed her mouth in a hard kiss that separated her from reality. As he ground his pelvis into hers, he lifted her up, and she locked her legs around his waist as his shaft pumped, and warmth filled her core. Completely spent, she collapsed against him, and he did the same to her until they were draped against the bookshelf, panting.

"I don't know what to think," she whispered. "I'm not certain I can walk just now." And what a lovely feeling that was!

"That is the best compliment a man can have," he said whispered back, as he pressed his lips to her forehead.

You'll know the man who is for you when he kisses your forehead for no reason…

The words that her father had given her, seemingly a lifetime ago, suddenly swam through the haze of her mind. The gesture was unexpected, even from him, but did it mean that? As a tiny piece of her heart went unexpectedly into his keeping, panic rose in her chest. *Oh, no!* She couldn't fall for a rake, not even one she enjoyed bantering with. Surely, he wouldn't be true to her, and he was younger besides. Then there was her brother to consider.

Stop thinking, Diana. You needn't figure everything out just now.

Eventually, her heartbeat returned to normal, and her breathing evened. When she came back to her senses, she pushed at Nathaniel's chest until he released her. When her feet hit the floor, she continued to shove at him until there was a fair amount of space between them.

"What now?" Since her legs felt like cooked porridge, she leaned into the bookshelf, careful to avoid the volumes on the floor.

"Come lie with me for a bit. Then, when our strength returns, I'll drive you home." As he spoke, the viscount led her over to the sofa. He stretched out and moved to his side. When she joined him, she lay facing him.

A sigh left her throat. With her head resting in the crook of his elbow and his other arm slung about her hips and the warmth of his body seeping into hers, she basked in the aftereffects of intimacy. "It's lovely laying here with you. My husband never wished to linger in my bed. As soon as the deed was done, he left for his own suite." Or his mistress, depending on his mood.

"Some men have no idea of the treasure they have, and it's not about coin or jewels," he said in a low, rumbling voice that sent flutters through her chest.

For long moments, silence reigned between them. As he closed his eyes, she contented herself with exploring his body with her fingertips. There were a few scars of varying sizes and shapes on his back, and she delighted in the spattering of freckles she found here and there over his skin that she hadn't seen before.

"Tell me about your early days, before you became a rake, before you had your trust in women broken."

A soft grin curved his lips. When he opened his eyes, he

pinned her with his mossy green gaze. "Usually, by this time, I'm dressing myself in preparation for leaving a woman's bed."

"If you don't wish to talk, we don't need to." But she didn't wish to hear about his former lovers.

"No, it's not that. I… I rather like it." He encouraged a shock of her hair to curl around his finger. "When your brother went to join the war effort, I told him I didn't want to go with him. It was the first time we didn't do something together since Eton. I just couldn't go, Diana; I was terrified of being maimed or even killed." When he paused, she brushed the hair from his forehead. "I didn't want to kill other men merely because they weren't English. I mean, Napoleon was a horrid person and a dictator bent on world domination, but other countries' leaders aren't any better."

Fair point. "How did you keep busy instead? I'll wager your decision wasn't a popular one within your friend set."

"It wasn't." He snapped his gaze to hers again. "You truly want to know?"

"Yes." Oddly, she wished to know more about him. Yes, he was lovely as a carnal partner, but there was an attachment between them that went beyond that.

"I went to the Continent. I studied the works of writers, poets, and painters. Then I discovered what set my soul on fire— poetry. I dug deep in that, chased it wherever that path led. Collected volumes and papers of poetry for what seemed like years." He drew a hand down her arm, leaving gooseflesh behind. "I traveled through Rome and the various regions in Italy. I traveled in Portugal until the armies sent my arse back home."

"What happened then?"

"Well, I wanted more poetry, to know more poets, to talk with them and find out what had inspired them to write those lines. I collected what I could find from England, even met living poets. It was one of the best things I'd ever done, and I was even inspired in my own life."

"To bed as many women as you could?"

"Of course not. That is a separate issue." Nathaniel tweaked her nose with a grin. "Studying poetry changed my life. It made me feel better about myself and the decisions I'd made."

How interesting. "Yet you've never written your own. Why?"

He shrugged, and the gesture was elegant enough that she wanted to feel his body moving against hers again. "Fear? Embarrassment? Not enough motivation or inspiration?"

"But you said that poetry sets your soul on fire." Admiration for him rose up another notch. "Unless your dalliances are stronger than what your soul needs, perhaps you should continue to pursue that."

"I don't know, honestly. I suppose I'll figure it out."

"You've never allowed any of your contemporaries to know this about you?" No matter how far she delved into her memories, she didn't remember William ever telling her that his best friend was a budding poet.

"I didn't know how, and at times I wanted to keep it to myself, like a dragon hoarding gold." A sheepish expression came over his face. "And I also didn't want my friends to make jest of me."

"Being a poet is a well-respected living."

"Perhaps, but it is also feast or famine where income is concerned."

"And you have responsibilities." It wasn't a question.

"There is that."

Eventually, he would marry, and that would put an end to their budding affair. "Well, don't wait too long to pen your own lines, Nathaniel. You might be keeping real talent from the world."

"I appreciate the support. I..." His swallow was audible. "I haven't had that in a long time."

It seemed they were well-matched in more than a few ways. Not wanting to think about that either, Diana closed her eyes and let herself relax for the first time in a long while. Being bedded by a man who had quite the talent for intercourse had been amazing.

Never had she felt so sated or content.

In this moment, it was enough. Tomorrow could take care of itself.

CHAPTER NINE

April 29, 1817
Atterbury House
Grosvenor Square
Mayfair, London

A POUNDING ON her bedroom door woke Diana the next morning. With a yawn, she opened her eyes. Soft illumination lay behind the closed drapes, and when she glanced at the carriage-style clock on her bedside table, she groaned, for it was a tick past the hour of nine.

She frowned and hoped whoever was on the other side of the door would go away. With a sigh, she flopped back against her pillows, for she'd arrived home last night around two in the morning. Why? Because she'd drifted off to sleep on the viscount's sofa. They'd awoken at one, where he then had the cheeky idea to manipulate her body with his fingers and mouth until she'd fallen over the edge one more time. He'd laughed when she said she wanted to melt into the leather of the sofa.

But it had been true. How the man knew where to touch her so that she'd separate herself from reality, she had no idea, but she had no complaints with his performance. After that, they'd dressed and he'd driven her home in the rain.

When the pounding on her door intensified, she uttered a huff, pushed herself upward against her pillows, and pulled the bedclothes to her chin. "Come in."

As soon as the door swung inward, her brother pushed into her room. "Diana."

"William?" She gasped, for she suspected she knew why he was there, and her chest tightened. "Is it Papa?"

"I'm afraid so." As he spoke, he came closer to her bed. "He passed peacefully in his sleep about an hour ago, according to Mama. She was by his side until the last. When I awoke this morning, she told me."

"Oh." A twinge of guilt went through her as her stomach dropped. "I should have been there. Even though I'd seen him yesterday afternoon, I shouldn't have gone to the ball last night…"

"Hush, Sis. You can't think like that." William sat on the side of her bed. "I went to the ball as well, remember."

Honestly, she'd forgotten, for being with Nathaniel had made her forget… everything.

He continued. "Papa had been in a bad state for a while. We all knew it, and we all spent the time with him, but there was nothing wrong with living our lives while it was happening."

"Thank you for that." Still, an ache set up around her heart. "Did Meredith arrive yet?"

"She did." William nodded as he looked at her with compassion in his eyes. "Late last night, so she was able to say her goodbyes to Papa. So did her children. They came over straightaway after settling into her husband's townhouse."

A modicum of relief went down Diana's spine. "That's good. I'd hoped my children would have been here as well, but perhaps the road conditions are ragged from the rain."

"I know." He touched her hand, and she appreciated that bit of humanity and connection. "No doubt they'll come today. Mama will appreciate that. And it will be lovely having the whole family gathered. Papa would have been pleased."

Slowly, she nodded. Perhaps she should have summoned the children earlier, but there was no point in berating herself. "What happens now?"

"There will be a funeral, of course, that will need planning. Papa wanted to be buried on the Surrey property where his parents are at their final rest."

"That makes sense. Are we all going out there?"

"Not if it continues to rain. I thought I'd take Papa out there myself, with Mama if she wants to say her final goodbyes. It's my right as his son and now as the new earl." His expression turned somber. "Perhaps I'll ask Nathaniel to come out with me."

"Oh?" The sound of the viscount's name sent a few flutters in her lower belly. "Why is that?" Would he know she'd been with the man for the past few days?

"He's my best friend. I realize that I need him in this moment." His voice broke. "He's a good sort, you know?"

She was beginning to see that for herself. "He must be if you wanted Meredith to marry him instead of the man she's been in love with forever."

"Don't remind me." At least he appeared chagrined. "It was a hope, nothing more, to have him as a brother."

How interesting. "Then you think highly of him as a friend?"

"Well, he's a good man. Can't keep his prick in his breeches, but some men don't have the capabilities to remain true to one woman."

That didn't bode well for the future, did it? "Then you think he would be a terrible husband?"

"I didn't say that, exactly." William frowned as he met her gaze. Did he suspect anything? "Nate is the type of man that when he falls for a woman, he falls wholeheartedly—lock, stock, and barrel. However, I've yet to see him meet a woman who captivates him on all levels, so that he would consider changing his current lifestyle."

Of course, William didn't know everything. Still, heat went through her cheeks. "It might happen. Hasn't he already indicated an interest in marrying?"

"He has, so it might." His shrug only lifted one shoulder. "Regardless, I'll keep you informed of plans as Mama and I make them."

"Thank you." She felt far too numb just now and couldn't summon tears.

As he stood, her brother turned and stared at her. "By the by, where were you during the later part of the ball?"

Oh, dear. Her pulse kicked up. "What do you mean?"

"I didn't see you after a while, and I wanted to introduce you to a man who might be good for you for a second husband."

Icy fingers played her spine. Yes, she'd returned to society for that exact purpose, but now that she'd agreed to an affair with Nathaniel, did she want to curtail what had barely gotten started to secure her future? "Oh, I was talking to friends in the corridors, and then I found myself fatigued, for I'd forgotten how strenuous being in society is. Lord Holdcraft came by and offered to take me home so I wouldn't need to wait for you or interrupt your enjoyment."

"Ah." Slowly, he nodded as an expression of puzzlement crossed his face. Could he see through the lie? Would he continue to question her? "That makes sense. I'll send a note 'round to Nathaniel and let him know about Papa. He'll probably wish to call on both Mama and you." Then his gaze alighted on the floral bouquet she'd brought into her room and put on the dresser. "Do you have a suitor you're keeping from me?"

Another round of heat went through her cheeks. "I do not. Just hopeful young pups. You know how they are with gifts."

"Right." He nodded, and relief coursed down her spine. "Come have dinner with Mama and the family tonight. She'll need us all around her now more than ever."

"I promise that I will." And eventually, she'd need time to grieve for herself.

TRUE TO FORM, and just as William had foretold, Nathaniel came to call later that afternoon. He brought another bouquet, this one of more demure blooms in whites, lavender, baby pinks, and she received him in the drawing room.

"I appreciate your intent to call. I'm still shocked by the news," Diana said as she brought the bouquet to her nose. The soft floral scent oddly brought her comfort.

"How could I not? I just came from William's house." Sadness clouded his eyes as he met her gaze. "You have my condolences regarding your father."

"Thank you." Carefully, she set the flowers on an ivory-inlaid occasional table as early stages of grief fluttered around her heart. "Life is going to look so different now."

He nodded. "William asked me to accompany him to Surrey when he's ready to bury your father."

"He said he would ask. Will you go?" Suddenly, the thought of him being gone caused hot panic to rise in her chest. Surely, she hadn't grown into one of those women to grow too dependent on a man.

"That depends."

She frowned. "On what?"

"Will you go also?" The tiny bit of hope on his face was adorable.

"Willaim said I shouldn't, said the rain will rut the roads. No doubt he doesn't wish for all of us to endure such a trip." For the space of a few heartbeats, she remained quiet. "However, I would imagine if the weather is clear for the days taken with planning, there will be a procession from London to Surrey. Papa was well known and well loved. Then I will go."

"Fair enough." As Nathaniel nodded, a frown tugged at the corners of his sensual mouth. "I don't know his timeline for such things. When my parents died, I remember laying them to rest quietly and without fanfare in the same year, but it took a toll on my psyche."

"Death is always lurking." She pressed her lips together. "I'd imagine William will have Papa laid out in the parlor for mourners for a couple of days after the undertaker does his job.

We'll all have to dye dresses and gowns, and then within the week, everyone will remove to Surrey for the burial. Papa never wished to make a fuss in life, so I don't guess his death will be any different. The funeral service will be short. Since it's private on his estate, I'll attend if I feel up to it."

"Your father was a lovely man, someone I aspired to be had I gone down the same path as him. Much different from my own father."

When a pained expression crossed his face, concern for him grew inside her. "What else is troubling you?"

"Honestly, I'd rather not be parted from you when we've only just started our affair."

The fact he didn't shy away from that truth impressed her. And her traitorous heart skipped a beat. "Surrey isn't far from London. At best, we'll be parted for a week or two, and if I *do* come to the country, some of that time can be spent together."

Though his face brightened, he heaved a sigh. "With far too many people about."

Despite the subject matter, she chuckled. "I know." Even now, when sadness battered her insides, her body reacted to having him so close. "All will be well, and if you as a gentleman, can't make room for what happens in life, if you think that the act of living inconveniences your selfish intentions, then you aren't the man I thought you were."

Did that mean she was coming to care for him more than she should?

"I am only feeling selfish because I've just realized what a wonderful person you are." Yet he nodded and held her gaze. "I should go. I told William I'd help with any preparations he needs, and though he might not show it, he'll break, and soon."

"He will, but I think he's the strongest of us all at times." A lump of tears lodged in her throat. "Regardless, you are a good man, Nathaniel. Never think you're not or that you're less than others, somehow."

He nodded. "Thank you."

"Will you come to dinner at William's? Mama would appreciate seeing you, I think, and spending time with you."

"I will."

"My children should arrive today, hopefully. Would you like to meet them?" It was an offer she didn't extend to just anyone, but she oddly trusted this man.

Surprise jumped into his eyes. "For you? Of course."

"Good." Somehow, the words made her feel far too vulnerable, for her husband never put her needs into consideration. If her father had died while she'd been married to him, he would have said he'd be with his mistress and to write when everything was over. Tears welled in her eyes. Nathaniel was immediately concerned and closed the distance between them. "I'm going to miss my father so much. I hadn't seen him as much as I'd liked what with the demands on my time and the children's needs, but he always wrote to me while I was in the country, until he got sick. He was the backbone of our family. What will happen now?" Not knowing the answer, the tears overflowed onto her cheeks, and before she knew it, she'd broken down into a watering pot.

"Aw, sweeting." He was there with his arms around her, holding her as she cried into his cravat. Had he realized the endearment had slipped out? "Everything will come out right in the end. William has been given the honor of being your family's backbone now, and he's been readying himself for just that since your father fell ill." As he slipped a hand up and down her back, there was comfort in the simple gesture. "I'm sure he'll manage to surprise you."

She sniffled. "Why is there so much death in life?" No, she still wasn't broken about her husband's demise two years ago, but it had been a sad moment because of her children.

"It's the price we pay, I think. Love isn't given without some sort of promise, and neither is life. There is always death to pay, which is why we should make the best use of our time." His voice caught, and the subtle sound had her pulling slightly away to find his gaze with hers.

"What?"

He shook his head. Sadness and regret warred for dominance in those mossy pools. "Your father's passing has made me think about things."

"How so?"

"I've been a nodcock, Diana. Wasted much of my life on shallow, stupid, things that don't matter." A long-suffering sigh left his throat. "I should have married long ago, had children. Now time is running out. It might be too late for me to make my mark or leave a legacy. Hell, even have my family name live on."

Unfortunately, that was true, which was why he needed to marry a younger woman. That meant there could be nothing substantial between her and him beyond the affair. But she wanted to reassure him. "No, it's not. Emotions are exacerbating things." Once more, she clung to him, for there was security and safety in his arms. "Don't leave just yet. Please?"

He tightened his hold ever so slightly. "I'm here for as long as you need."

When he kissed her forehead, Diana crumpled in his hold and cried even harder, for her father had told her long, long ago that she'd know the man meant for her by his forehead kisses and how he treated her in moments of adversity. Atterbury never did that, and it was something her father had always done to her mother that Diana had thought so dear.

She'd wanted that in her own marriage, but had been bitterly disappointed.

"Shh. It will be well enough," he whispered as he seemed content enough to hold her, let her cry out her initial grief on his shoulder.

It was beyond soothing. Was Nathaniel meant for her, then? Now was not the time to think about that. For the moment, there was only her and him. Questions could wait.

CHAPTER TEN

May 12, 1817
Sammerson House
St. James's Place   ·
Mayfair, London

IT HAD BEEN fourteen days since Nathaniel had brought Diana a bouquet of flowers upon hearing the news that her father had died, and it had been five days since he'd seen her at all.

Everyone in the Sammerson family had gone to Surrey three days after the earl's death, for the weather had proved decent enough. In accordance to how well liked the earl was, his funeral procession from London to his Northfield Hall in Surrey was quite large, made up of family, friends, and acquaintances.

Since there had been an extraordinary number of mourners, Nathaniel offered to open his manor for overflow guests who were staying multiple nights. It was the right thing to do, and because his property bordered William's, it was easy to convey people to and fro. He didn't mind taking on the additional expense of housing and feeding them either; it was the least he could do for William and Diana.

In fact, the whole experience changed him, proved a turning point of sorts. After watching them both interact with all the people, after seeing them pull close to the family—and the fact they included him in that—he wanted such close connections for himself. No longer did he want to live a scattered life full of empty liaisons, never being important to anyone.

So he'd thrown himself wholeheartedly into caring for the Sammerson family, making certain that his best friend had the easiest time he could of conducting the funeral and finally laying the earl to rest. In this way, perhaps he could show Diana that not all men were bounders like her husband had been.

Eventually, the gathering ended. When the first of the mourners and supporters left Surrey, Diana and her children—with whom he'd spent a decent amount of time—returned to London. Shortly after, her sister Meredith and her family went back to their country estate.

Nathaniel stayed on to assist with the cleanup and to lend moral support to his best friend. Eventually, William and the dowager countess left after the remainder of the guests and mourners returned home. Only then did Nathaniel prepare to travel back to London. He had business there after all, and he was anxious to see Diana again.

Damn. What does it mean that I've been lost without her?

With a shuddering sigh, and the shake of his head, Nathaniel wrenched himself out of his thoughts. He peered out the window of his closed carriage. Of course it was raining, when wasn't it? Would Diana be there as well? The possibility of seeing her after the past two weeks of pure chaos tightened his chest and sent interest shivering through his shaft. Would she wish to continue the affair that had barely begun? God, he hoped so, for he needed her in his life for more than just the carnal.

And that surprised the hell out of him.

A tap on the roof preceded his driver announcing they were arriving at their destination.

"Thank you." He rubbed a gloved hand along the side of his face then he adjusted the collar of his greatcoat upward so the rain wouldn't drip down the back of his neck. Once the vehicle rocked to a halt and then dipped when the driver hopped down from his bench, a heavy sigh escaped Nathaniel's throat. As the door opened and his driver put down the steps, he nodded. "No doubt I'll be here a bit. Go on home and get out of the rain. When I'm ready to leave, I'll send a summons."

"As you like, my lord."

Ten minutes later, after he'd given over his damp outer things to the footman at the door, the butler led him up to the drawing room and announced him.

A frown tugged his lips downward, for the only person occupying the room was the dowager countess. "I've come to see William. Is he at home?"

She glanced up from the handiwork in her lap. "He is, but he's talking with his man-of-affairs in his study. He'll be along shortly."

"I see." Not knowing what to do, he bounced his gaze between her and the door. "Do you mind if I spend time with you?"

"Not at all." Lady Northfield set aside her embroidery. "Come sit near to me, Holdcraft. We haven't had time to speak privately since my husband died. The last weeks have proved far too busy and exhausting, to tell the truth."

"Such is life, I'm afraid." He dropped into a chair near the sofa where she sat. All the furniture was upholstered in mauve-and-gold brocade to match the same colors in the wallpaper. Would William redecorate once he was confirmed as earl? "How do you fair, Lady Northfield?"

"I honestly believe it depends on the hour." Sadness pooled in her eyes that were so much like Diana's. "It's a whole new way of learning how to order my days. Even though we knew Northfield's time was coming, I didn't truly expect there to be such a hole in my life after his passing." She shook her head. "We'd been married such a long time, I don't know how I'm to go forward now."

When the sound of tears threatened in her voice, he leaned over and patted her hand. "I can't imagine how you must be feeling. Will you remain in London with William?"

"For a bit," she said with a watery-eyed nod. "I need William's strength just now, and since Diana is in Town while her son adjusts to the demands of his new title, I'll have her to spend time with as well."

At the mention of her name, his heart skipped a beat. Need twisted down his spine to lodge in his stones. There'd not been time for them to slip away and be together carnally during the past two weeks, and he'd quite missed her. Not just for the physical. Her presence in his life had offered a lightness and a purpose of sorts that he'd become almost reliant on in that short amount of time.

Then he cleared his throat. "Your children are strong and independent. You and Northfield did well in that regard. Frankly, I admired the earl and how he ordered his life."

"He was a good man." She flicked her gaze over his face. "And you have always been a charmer, Holdcraft." Then she pinned him with a speculative look. "Is there a woman in your life? William mentioned that you needed to marry more sooner than later."

"Oh." Heat crept up the back of his neck. "Let us say there is perhaps the *thought* of one, but nothing has moved in that direction as of yet." Did he even want Diana past an affair? Such as it was with the interruption? Was he truly thinking along matrimonial lines?

"You are far too old to still be sowing wild oats."

"I know." For the space of a few heartbeats, he thought carefully over his next words. "If I'm being honest, this time with your family has made me think that perhaps I should do something about my life merely to have others around me. I…" As a wad of emotion lodged in his throat, he cleared it. "I don't want to reach the end of my life and have no one there to care that I'll soon be gone."

"Understandable. I'm glad you are coming to your senses." It was her turn to pat his hand. "I imagine it's stressful knowing you need to do your duty to the title."

"There is that. I'm thinking about that more with each passing day." Yet if he *did* choose Diana for a wife, if all the stars aligned and that was suddenly possible, she was of an age that she was too old to bear children. He might have the wife but there would still be no offspring, and certainly no heir to inherit the title. What would happen then?

"Well, you still have your looks, and they will serve you well when selecting a wife among the eligible women within the *ton* right now."

The thought of having to do the pretty for only God knew how long, courting women far younger than himself, and possibly not liking any of them for his future wife nearly turned his stomach. Truth to tell, he didn't want another woman beyond Diana.

Yet she wasn't his, either.

The dowager sniffled. She dabbed at the corners of her eyes with a handkerchief that had a black ribbon sewn around the edges. "By the by, Diana has seemed different these past two weeks. Did you have cause to notice?"

Ah, when he watched her from afar every second that he could? "Losing a parent will do that." *Perhaps the separation between us had been a good thing.* It slowed their relationship down and allowed them both time to think. For his part, he wanted her more than ever, but if commonsense crept in, did she regret agreeing to an affair?

"No, it's beyond that, I think."

"What?" He snapped his attention back to the dowager.

She nodded. "It's almost as if my daughter has a secret, as if she's found someone for her life who makes her truly happy."

"Has she?" Shock slammed into his chest. Why didn't he notice?

"Oh, yes. I saw it in her eyes that she looked forward to re-turning to London, probably to see him again. Do you know anything about that?" There was a shrewdness to her glance.

"Uh…" Nathaniel froze. Did she suspect? "I'm afraid I don't."

She tsked her tongue. "I have known you for as long as I've known my own son." Her eyes were kind if tired as she held his gaze. "When you were a young man, before Diana wed and before you went away to the Continent, you were once sweet on her regardless that she is five years older than you."

Bloody hell. She *did* suspect! What to say now? He cleared his throat. "That was in the past."

"Mmm, I rather doubt anything has changed for you. Oh, perhaps you were thwarted in love over the course of your life; most men are. And that is why you've built the walls of a rake around yourself, to try and protect your heart, but you have never forgotten Diana." One of her graying eyebrows lifted in question. "Is that true?"

How could this woman possibly see through him with such ease? Sweat rolled down his spine to plaster his lawn shirt to his back. Several heartbeats passed before he finally nodded. "What if I haven't?"

The dowager shrugged. "There is no sin in wanting an older woman, Holdcraft, and you make a handsome couple together."

Another shock slammed into him. "Do you, ah, know what happened between Diana and me recently?" Every word he spoke came with heat on his neck that climbed toward his ears. Surely, she would see that damning flush.

The dowager's eyes twinkled. "No, she hasn't said a word, but I suspected. Her notice was never far from you when we were together for the mourning party."

Was that so? How interesting. "And?" He could barely breathe from anticipation.

"It is good to know there is a man who wishes to protect her, to look after her, and treat her in the way she should have been treated by Atterbury." As her eyes narrowed, Nathaniel wondered just how much Diana had told her mother about her marriage. "I was opposed to that match, but my husband insisted. He said it would do her good to marry the viscount."

"I beg your pardon, but that was a nodcock idea."

"Oh, I won't argue with you on that. Diana often wrote to me of how lonely she was. She asked many times if things would grow better between her and Atterbury, or if he might drop his mistress and see her worth as a wife."

God, that was heartbreaking, and still shock tightened his chest. "I'm sorry to hear that."

"So was I, and how could I, as her mother, assure her of something I knew would never occur?"

That must have been difficult from every perspective. "Yet you haven't objected to me."

"Why should I? You have been there for her, I suspect, for many things since you came back into her life."

If he was hit by any more shock, he might just be knocked off his chair. "You wouldn't oppose a possible match between us? That is, *if* I prove to be the marrying type?"

"Ha!" The dowager snorted. "At this stage of life? No, I wouldn't. Everyone deserves happiness and someone who cares for us unconditionally. If you've found that with her and she with you, who am I to oppose it?" She paused and once more patted his hand. "I've always liked you, Nathaniel. Since you have been friends with William for such a long time, I know you are loyal. However, I don't like the lifestyle you lead, but I'm confident that will change once you find yourself in love."

Love. Was it even possible after all this time? After he'd been thwarted by it twice in the past? He didn't know, but oddly he hoped that these feelings were what he was beginning to feel for Diana. It was certainly different than the infatuation he'd had for her as an untried youth. The best way he could explain what he currently felt was the sensation of being home.

Realizing the dowager waited on his answer, he asked, "You won't tell William?" A bit of relief made its way through his gut to finally have this knowledge out in the open. Along with it came excitement that buzzed at the base of his spine. Was this the path he'd wanted to tread for such a long time without knowing it?

A small chuckle came from the lady. "I will not, for that is *your* responsibility. However, conduct your liaison discreetly, as we *are* in mourning."

"Of course." Had he just been given permission to court Diana? Did he want to try? There was much to think about before he saw her next. "Thank you, Lady Northfield. I'll strive to be worthy of you both."

She nodded, and once more, her eyes filled with tears. "However…"

"Yes?" Nathaniel braced for whatever else she would say.

Her eyes bored into his. "Don't hurt her. If you think to merely use her and trifle with her affections like you've done with the string of other women over the years, I *will* put my foot down and have William run you off." Her lips formed a tight line. "I don't care about your friendship with him. My daughter deserves only good things now, not men after their own pleasures."

Properly chastised, he nodded. "I quite agree, and you have my word. I have no intention of hurting Diana." Should he reveal more of a personal nature to her? Deciding it might help his suit, he added, "In fact, I think I'm coming to care for her more than is good for me, but there is much to decide between us, and I need time to order my thoughts."

"Very well." She reached over and grasped his hand. "If you do decide to come up to scratch, speak with her son. Percy has a right to be informed if a man wishes to marry his mother."

Fuck. It was all happening so fast that it was frightening. First though, he needed to reconnect with Diana, find out how she'd gotten on since the funeral, but he nodded. "I'll take that under advisement, and thank you for the opportunity for this chat."

"Good luck, Holdcraft. I hope she leads you a merry chase, for I have a feeling you'll bedevil her as well. That sort of relationship will have the roots to last."

Damn, he wanted to believe her, but he was ages away from finding out.

Chapter Eleven

Later that evening

THE LONGCASE CLOCK in the corridor outside the dining room at her parents' townhouse—now her brother's, really—struck the seventh hour. That sound seemed to echo in her soul, and with a start, Diana realized how much she'd missed Nathaniel over the past two weeks.

Of course, there was a hole in her soul from the absence of her father, and she would always miss him, but she was done with being a watering pot all the time. Right now, she wanted something to distract her from the grief, and that could only be achieved by seeing the viscount.

Did she dare to go searching for Nathaniel? Would her family question her whereabouts?

Once dinner concluded, she made her excuses as if it were the most natural thing in the world. Both her children had plans for the evening in the way of societal events, and since she didn't wish to go home and sit in the silence, spending time with Holdcraft felt like just the thing.

William frowned as he stood up from the table. "I can drive you home if you wish."

"That isn't necessary. I'll take my carriage then send it back for Percy's use." As she spoke, Diana smiled at her son, who nodded. "It's been so busy these past two weeks, I haven't had time to myself or to think. I'm looking forward to the quiet." It wasn't all a lie, but the statement wasn't the full truth either.

Eliza rested her gaze on Diana. "Do you wish for me to come home with you, Mama? I can forego being with my friends if you wish for company."

Oh, dear.

"Don't be silly. I intend to snuggle into bed, perhaps spend an hour or two reading before retiring." Another half-truth, for though she would be in a bed of sorts, it wasn't for reading or relaxing. If the viscount was of a mind, she would convince him to thoroughly claim her body.

Percy nodded. "Be well, Mama. I probably won't be home until well after midnight."

"Enjoy the time with your friends, both of you, but don't do anything scandalous. You are in mourning, after all," she told her children. They needed that social interaction and to make connections in order to grow into adults.

Her mother said nothing, only looked at her with speculation, that left Diana with questions.

With nothing for it, by the time she went downstairs for her spencer, gloves, and bonnet, the closed carriage had arrived at the curb. Using her driver's assistance, she gave him Nathaniel's address in Bedford Square and managed not to blush as she seated herself on a bench inside. Her nerves felt strung too tight as the vehicle lurched into motion. Why was she so nervous? She was a widow, for heaven's sake, and she had the freedom to do whatever she wanted, but calling on a man—her lover—was in a different realm entirely.

"I don't care," she whispered to herself as she gazed out the window. "I need this; I need... *him.*" Did that make her weak or dependent?

Upon arrival, she was admitted into the house without incident. The same butler she'd seen from the last time she had been there left her in a downstairs parlor with a look of curiosity. Then he left, presumably to speak with Lord Holdcraft. After a few moments, the butler returned. He showed her into the library on the first level, told her the viscount would join her directly and did she want tea.

"Yes, please. I'm a bit chilled, for May has been damp." And it would fortify her courage to seduce the viscount if needed. Then she sighed and breathed in deeply. The scent of leather, old books, ink, and dust was soothing to her soul. The bookshelves beckoned in the low illumination from the few candles lit about the room.

But she refrained from exploring in favor of sitting on a low sofa of impossibly buttery-soft leather. The tea service arrived before the viscount did. Perhaps that was a good thing, for by the time she'd poured out and fixed her cup and indulged, her nerves were a bit more settled. When Nathaniel came into the room and shut the door, her heart leapt. She quickly put the cup and saucer on the table and stood.

"Nathaniel." The word left her throat on a choked whisper; she hadn't realized how much she'd wanted to see him.

"Diana." Then he was there without a word, taking her into his arms and merely holding her, and it was exactly what she craved after everything she'd been through the past two weeks.

After a few moments, with tears in her eyes, she pulled back and peered into his face. The caring mixed with desire in his mossy gaze made her quite breathless. "I missed you." There was no shame in the admission.

"In a physical capacity?" Amusement danced in his eyes, but the deep rumble of his voice tickled through her chest and sent awareness sailing over her skin.

"Yes, but also in other ways as well." She laid a palm on his hard chest, and it was all she could do not to pounce or push him onto the sofa. "Being here with you tonight is a balm, and I thank you for it."

He cupped her cheek, caressed his fingers along the side of her neck while his hungry gaze roved over her face. "I'm glad you're here because I've missed you too, but didn't want to intrude on your family time."

"It wouldn't have been an intrusion." Yet her heart skipped a beat, for he was so sweet. All she wanted to do was tumble into his arms and let him protect her from the sadness of the world. Then she remembered that she had something for him. "I brought you a gift."

"Oh?" Surprise jumped into his expression. "Why?"

"You were on my mind when I was out shopping for black ribbon and other accessories the other day." With regret, she moved away to pull a slim volume from her reticule. "When I couldn't find a memento for you in the shops, I found it while perusing through Papa's library. Oddly, he had a collection of Keats's poems, though it's not the whole battery of work you wanted. These are merely poems that are popular in society right now. You might already have a copy, though."

"Ah, Diana." Gratitude lay stamped on his face when he took the blue linen-covered book with silver lettering. "This is lovely. Thank you. And I don't have this volume." He opened the book, flipped through a few pages. "God, it contains the poem I've wanted." When he looked at her, gratitude and something else she couldn't identify reflected in his eyes. "This is wonderful." He set the book on a nearby occasional table. "*You* are wonderful, and I fully intend to read you that poem soon."

"I'm glad you like it."

"So much, but I adore the fact that you are here more." Seconds later, Nathaniel tugged her into his arms again, and he kissed with such intention as if he hadn't seen her in a lifetime.

Not that she minded. Diana returned his embrace with enthusiasm. In this man, she could forget the sadness of losing her father, but also, he had given her back the pieces of herself she'd lost during her less than satisfactory marriage with Atterbury. Overwhelming need for him fell over her.

"Tonight, I wish to be wild and abandoned, and I want you, Nathaniel." If that admission made her vulnerable, so be it, but it was true.

With a growl, the viscount walked her backward toward one

of the shelves and a wooden ladder attached to the shelf on a track on the ceiling. "In this, you and I are in agreement." He nuzzled the spot where her neck joined her shoulder. "Never feel embarrassed for what you need, what your body requires."

"With you, I don't. Oddly enough." She offered no resistance when he tugged down her bodice. All too quickly, her breasts popped free of the layers of fabric, and she yearned to feel his hands on them, for the relatively cool ambient air wafted across her already sensitive, hardened nipples. Slowly, she was going mad. "Nathaniel, please."

"Please what?" He kneaded those mounds of flesh, rolled the stiff buds at their root, and she involuntarily arched her back. "Please continue? As if I would stop, for I've dreamed of having you in my bed over the past two weeks." The viscount followed his words with a line of heated kisses beneath her jaw.

Perhaps they were both depraved, but she didn't care. He made her feel more herself than she'd ever been. Heightened desire smacked into her like a wave. Diana slid her hands up his chest to rest on his shoulders. "Mmm."

"So beautiful you can inspire the poets." The viscount plucked those tips, rubbed his fingers over them with varying degrees of friction until she panted and bit her bottom lip to keep from crying out, begging him for more.

His whispered words in that jungle-cat purr, coupled with the wicked torture he produced, left her shaking with need. "Then you should definitely put pen to paper, but leave my name out of it." Of its own violation, her head lolled back to rest against his shoulder, and he chuckled as if he knew exactly what she was going through.

"Perhaps I will." He again rolled the nipples, flicked those nubs, and with each new round of pressure, heat throbbed between her thighs. "I'll wager more poetry has been inspired due to women like you, women who don't shy away from life, who feel deep due to their experiences."

"I don't know..." A shiver of want shot down her spine. If he didn't cease, she'd collapse at his feet, or either succumb to an attack of the heart for her pulse raced erratically. Frankly, she welcomed all he would make her feel.

"I'll prove you wrong, then." The longer he grazed her nipples with his palms, crushed her breasts together as he caressed them, the more the unrelenting pressure for more built and stacked low in her belly. His lips were at the shell of her ear. "Should I make my poetry, my words, erotic, I wonder? You inspire that in me as well."

"Such gammon." She squeaked with pleasure when he gave her nipples a light pinch that left her reeling with twin threads of decadence and lovely pain cycling through her body.

Diana sagged against the shelf, trapped between them and this man as she gave herself over to his care. She was as limp as cooked porridge already, and all he'd done was play at her breasts. The more she tried to gather her composure, the more she was shaken at her intense reaction from his teasing as well as her own blatant need for more.

"Let us move to the next stage of this night, hmm?" The gleam in his moss-green eyes meant trouble for her as he moved her to the ladder.

"I wished to seduce you, though."

"Then you should have established that from the outset."

Trapped between his arms and the ladder, Diana's pulse pounded as he peppered her nape with feather-weighted kisses. "Not fair." Each time his lips and fingers glanced over her skin, her willpower dissolved into dust.

More of her cares melted away.

"All is fair in carnal games, my dear." He turned her around so that she faced the ladder then slowly, he drew up her black taffeta skirting while nuzzling into the crook of her shoulder.

When her sensitized nipples grazed one of the ladder's wooden rungs, a wave of desire swept over her. She bit her bottom lip to stifle an unexpected whimper. "Rake."

The viscount pulled her backside flush to his front. "There is a strong connection between us, and perhaps that is what I was before."

She frowned. "Before what?" Was it vain to want to hear him say the words?

"Before you." He snaked a hand around her hips, glanced it along her mons to furrow a finger through her feminine curls. "Let me in, Diana. I want you as much as you want me."

"Gladly, for I wasn't best pleased to have our affair interrupted."

Chuckling, he widened her stance with a knee. Then he glided his fingers along her flesh made slick from his teasing, back and forth in a mesmerizing rhythm, drawing forth her arousal. "I adore how primed you are." Before she could utter a response, he'd coaxed her swelling nubbin out of hiding, rubbing it.

Diana moaned. With each pass of those talented fingers, shivers of raw need fell over her, fracturing throughout her body into every nerve ending. Damn, how could he bring her that close to the edge without much effort?

"I can't remember the last time I met a woman who has completely arrested my life." Over and over, he worked that tiny bundle of nerves, and when she couldn't hold back another moan, he grinned, his lips sliding over her nape. "And I think you're a vixen in disguise, one who just needed the correct key to set you free."

"Perhaps," she managed to gasp out and curled her fingers around the side of the ladder merely to keep herself upright. Any second, she'd hurtle over that edge into bliss.

"Atterbury was an idiot. He wasted all that time, when he had the best of all women at his side. God, I wish he was alive so I could kill him for that." Just when she thought she'd break from the exquisite torment, Nathaniel withdrew his hand. He turned her about so that her arse lay perched on a wooden tread. Ragged desire reflected in his eyes. "He never deserved you."

"I know, but he is in the past, and I'd like to keep him there." She met his gaze. "No more teasing, Holdcraft. I need you." This was improper and outrageously scandalous. *His* name and reputation wouldn't be ruined if they were discovered in highly compromising positions. Yet that didn't prevent her from wanting everything he would give, everything they would explore together.

"I know exactly how you feel." Once more he drew up her skirting and bunched it at her waist. As he dropped to his knees, he grinned up at her. Then he gripped her inner thighs and splayed her open. "I could spend days paying tribute to your thighs, your feminine folds."

It wasn't poetry, but it had the same effect. The sensation of falling assailed her. She buried the fingers of one hand into his hair. "Nathaniel, I…" Her voice cut off in a squeak as he touched his mouth to her button.

He chuckled. The vibrations sent her into another level of delight and wonder. And he began the next stage of his seduction.

"Merciful heavens." From the moment he employed his lips and hot tongue to her most sensitive, private parts, Diana slowly lost the last vestiges of her sanity. "I've wanted you to do this since that first time…" She couldn't catch her breath, for with each nibble, every nip, all the swipes and strokes of his tongue, she was hurled higher and higher into pleasure where she'd ever gone before.

Wild sensation coursed through her body. She shook from it. Tears unashamedly fell to her cheeks for the feelings were too big, too much, too overwhelming, and they swept her soul clear of most of the sadness and hopelessness she'd felt in recent days. Never once did he shy away from his work. He was a man bent on tossing her over the edge, and she hovered there, trapped, waiting with held breath and a hammering heart for him to release her into that dark void.

Except that descent into release never came.

The wicked man kept her poised on the razor's edge, pinning her there again and again with every penetrating stroke of his tongue, each calculated nibble, every new torment of suction on that swollen button until she implored him to stop lest she perish from the sensations. She curled her hand into his hair alternately to shove him away and cease the exquisite torture, but also to hold him to her tighter exactly where she needed him.

Fearing she'd faint from the need threatening to tear her apart, Diana squirmed, but he gripped her thighs that much tighter to keep her in place on that dratted ladder. Only when she'd met him had she finally had her carnal needs met. She shook as tears of pleasure rolled down her cheeks. Her legs fell open wider as her back arched, which put her deeper into his care. She'd not managed to achieve such gratification with her own fingers as he gave her now.

"I'm nearly there." The rushed whisper was filled with blatant pleading, but she didn't care. He was everything she'd ever wanted in a lover. When he didn't appear to have heard her, she clutched the sides of the ladder above her head. "I need—Ah!"

The dam holding back the mounting pressure within broke. She shattered in spectacular fashion, fell into that black void full of the most wonderful bliss as her inner walls convulsed with a strong release. She threw back her head, opened her mouth, yet no sound emerged. That was how it was each time the viscount made her fly.

He glanced at her, but she was barely aware. "So beautiful," he said with a smug grin. "Perhaps I'm selfish, but I want you to spend again merely so I can watch."

"I don't think I can." Already, she was as limp as a wet rag.

"Oh, you will."

Despite the fact her body shook as if she'd shoot right off the ladder and launch through the rooftop, he continued to worry her swollen, hypersensitive button. When he inserted two fingers, pumping them in and out of her shuddering passage, she bucked against his hand while imagining those fingers were his length spearing into her. But then he twisted those digits in order to massage a spot on her spasming flesh that finished her off.

"Nathaniel!" The word was long and drawn out in a keening

wail. She couldn't even summon embarrassment from that utterance, for she hurtled over the edge into a hard release that stole her breath and rendered her temporarily unable to move. Her thighs trembled in time to her racing pulse, while strong contractions rocked through her. Finally, he withdrew, and she collapsed into the rungs of the ladder, uncaring that the hard wood dug into her skin or that she most likely resembled a broken doll.

"I adore seeing you come undone and knowing that it was me who sent you to the stars." There was no mistaking the smugness in his voice.

Heat went through her cheeks, but she hadn't the strength to deny he had skill. "Amazing."

"We're not done yet, and I think you know it." The viscount removed a pristine handkerchief from an interior pocket. He watched her as he wiped the shiny moisture from his face. "Shall we continue?"

Unfulfilled longing circled through her body. Though he'd sent her flying, the urge to feel his body moving against—in— hers wouldn't quiet. "God, yes. It's why I originally came here tonight." Slowly, she peeled herself from the ladder. Her knees were decidedly wobbly, much to the viscount's amusement.

"If you can't stand, I've done my job well." He chuckled and the sound sent awareness into the areas he'd already made tingling. "Do you wish for proper or unorthodox?"

"As if what we've already done has been proper." She slipped her gaze down his body. The outline of his engorged member was clear in his buff-colored breeches. He was quite aroused, and she couldn't wait to feel that thick length inside her body. With a trembling smile, she let him lead her toward one of the leather sofas, but instead of laying her down, he urged her toward a bolstered end. "Nathaniel?"

"You'll enjoy this." Gently, and with the veriest tremble to his hand, he eased her upper half over the end. Seconds later, he shoved her skirting upward, bunching it at her waist. "Bid me nay, Diana, and I'll leave off."

Anticipation swamped her. "Claim me. I can wait no longer."

"I adore it when you beg," he said in a whisper as he leaned over her body while wrenching his frontfalls down. "But I adore even more the opportunity to fuck you senseless."

The leather against her palms as she sought to balance herself was in direct contrast to the heat in her blood. Awareness tingled through her when her erect nipples moved over the leather bolster, due to Nathaniel urging her legs apart. Gooseflesh rippled along her skin the second he gripped her hips, and an unexpected cry left her throat the moment the tip of his member glanced at her opening.

Before she could urge or beg him to join with him, he thrust inside her passage with such strength that every nerve ending she had lit up with pleasure, and he didn't stop until he was fully seated.

"Oh, God!" This was much different from the last time they'd coupled. At this angle and the way he'd penetrated her, the sensations were so intense she suspected she might go over the edge straightaway.

"Good, yes?" He gripped her hips more firmly, and she wondered if he'd leave finger-shaped bruises.

"Like the best French pastry or a well-aged bottle of champagne."

He leaned over and pressed his lips to her nape. "At least I'm in good, if expensive, company." Then he withdrew, and when she offered a whimpering protest, he chuckled and thrust back into her.

Their moans blended together.

The next few minutes were spent in wild, frantic intercourse. Each time he plunged into her passage, Diana pushed back against him as best she could, but it was difficult with her front half over the bolstered end of the sofa and her toes barely finding purchase on the floor.

Though he moved in and out like a man possessed, there was

also a gentleness to his strokes, an unspoken need to see her thoroughly pleasured, and that bonded her to him more than anything else. Tears welled in her eyes, for every thrust, every push sent her hurtling closer to the edge, but this physical act also showed her what life could be if she chose him for more than just an affair.

Deeper he drove, and faster his thrusts came. More frantic were his movements as he pressed against her, claiming her, keeping her trapped between his body and the bolster. Wave upon wave of pleasure slammed into her, urging her to let go, and when he groaned behind her, the sound unlocked the last of her inhibitions.

With a low cry of surrender, Diana fell into his care. Immediately, she broke, tumbled into a release that flew her to the stars and beyond. Bands of exquisite feeling rolled over her so intense that she was barely aware Nathaniel thrust twice more before following her into that special place where only lovers knew. The warmth of his release filled her core, and it was such an intimate, trusting act that she wanted to weep because of it.

How was it that in such a short time, she'd become completely enthralled with this man? In him, she was finding everything she'd wanted in another person, and she wanted him for more than just the bliss they shared while engaged in carnal games.

When her knees, her very bones, wouldn't support her weight any longer, Nathaniel pulled away. Seconds later, he guided her onto the sofa then wrapped his arms around her as they lay on their sides, her back flush against his front. Cuddling, being tucked into a nurturing, safe embrace following relations, was the ultimate exercise in bonding, for Atterbury always refused anything soft like this between them.

Another piece of her heart flew into Nathaniel's keeping. *I think I'm in a bit over my head.* There were worse things, though. "While I was in London and you were still in Surrey, one of the young bucks came to call on me." Why she chose now to tell him of this, she didn't know, but she didn't want misunderstandings between them.

Though he grunted, his hand tightened on her hip. "What did he want?"

Heat played in her cheeks. "To pay his addresses."

"The same man who wished to dance with you two weeks ago?"

"Yes."

"Damn, but I'm going to call him out. You are not for him."

"Ha." She couldn't help but snort even if his possessive nature amused her. "You don't own me, Nathaniel."

"No, but I thought what we have together is solid." A hint of vulnerability lingered in his voice, and it tugged at her heart.

"It is; don't you feel that connection between us?" When he remained silent, she went on. "However, what we have is only an affair. I can come and go as I please." Tears prickled in her throat, for wasn't that what she wanted from him? Then why was it suddenly not enough?

For long moments, the viscount was silent. Then he huffed. "Do you wish to encourage that man?"

She couldn't help a laugh. "Goodness, no. He's far too immature for me. I just wanted to mention it to you for full disclosure." Would it make him jealous enough to secure her future? She stifled a gasp. Did she *want* to marry him? Knowing his prior history and his affinity for bedding women, did that make her a fool?

"I appreciate that." Yet his body was still taut against hers.

Taking one of his hands, Diana brought it to her lips, pressed a kiss into his palm. "I don't wish to sink time into a man I'll need to train, and I certainly don't want to align myself with a man whose attention is divided instead of being on me." Was she trying to convince him or her? Did it matter? "Where is yours, Nathaniel?"

"On you. Always." The heat of his breath when he whispered warmed her cheek, the shell of her ear and he held her closer.

Her heart trembled. "I need to get home. I'd like to arrive

there before my children do."

"There is still time, I'll wager." As he spoke, Nathaniel brushed his fingers over her nipple, chuckling when it immediately responded to his touch. "Let me read one of Keats's poems to you, so you can understand why I like his work."

Another piece of heart flew into his keeping. *What am I going to do with you?* "I would like that."

CHAPTER TWELVE

May 13, 1817
Sammerson House
St. James's Place
Mayfair, London

THE NEXT EVENING, Nathaniel came 'round to the new Earl of Northfield's house, for his best friend had asked him over for dinner. Diana and her children would be in attendance, but he wished to talk to William beforehand.

After the time spent with Diana last night, he felt as if he could conquer the world. What they shared went beyond the usual empty trysts or one-night beddings. The more he found out about her, the more he wanted to know. What made her laugh? Did she have a favorite dessert? Which one of her nieces and nephews was her favorite? What was her favorite book?

Above all, would she consider spending far more time with him than a mere affair afforded?

As he came into the drawing room, Nathaniel cast a glance around the immediate area. As of yet, the only person there was William, and a swath of relief cut through his chest.

"Good evening, Northfield."

William grunted. "Not until my ascension to the title is confirmed by the powers that be, but I can't see an issue." Since he was at the sideboard, he poured out another glass of brandy and handed it to Nathaniel. "I'm glad you agreed to come to dinner with us again."

"Well, I consider you like my family." It was the truth. "Will your mother join us?"

"Unfortunately, she has retired early and wishes to have dinner on a tray in her room." He shrugged. "I think she's not feeling quite up to company."

"I can imagine the past two weeks have taken a toll on her. Or even perhaps longer than that, since your father was so sick for so long." Such a sobering thought, living with someone but knowing the whole time that they were dying before their eyes. He took a healthy sip of brandy and welcomed the burn of the liquor in his throat. "How are you doing, my friend?"

"Well enough." The answer was standardly noncommittal.

Nathaniel harumphed. "You don't need to be strong in front of me. I've known you since we were children and have known your father just as long. I know what he meant to you."

"There was no one like my father." As he spoke, William's expression crumbled a bit. Grief reflected in his eyes. "I miss him, feel that I didn't have enough time with him."

Another fact that was driven home to Nathaniel, and changing him from the inside out.

"What if I'm not as good an earl as he was?" William took a sip of his drink. "It's something I've labored under for more than a few years. Now that my father is gone, panic is my constant companion."

"I understand that particular anxiety, but that power is in your hands. If you want to be as good as your father, then do so." Growing up and being friends with William all their lives, he knew the training his friend had been given to prepare him for this very time in his life. "Your father has already given you the skills, taught you everything he knew. I know you can do this."

William eyed him from over the rim of his brandy glass. "God, when did you become the voice of reason? Of encouragement?"

"Your guess is as good as mine." Nathaniel shrugged and

saluted him with his brandy glass. "To the next Earl of North-field."

William lifted his own. "I'll have to be confirmed before I can officially take the title. It might take some time. You know this."

"I do, but it will eventually happen. You'll be the earl before the end of June when parliament breaks."

"Perhaps." Sadness flitted over William's features again. "How can I do this without my father?"

"We all feel like that, my friend, but we all must go our own ways eventually." Nathaniel clapped his free hand on William's shoulder. "I'll be there as well."

"Thank you." Silence reigned between them for more than a few moments before he spoke again. "Let us talk about something—anything—other than my being earl soon."

Nathaniel nodded, for he did have a purpose in coming here tonight beyond enjoying dinner with his best friend. "Very well. There *is* a topic I'd like to discuss." Had he truly summoned his courage to the sticking place?

"Come to think of it, you do appear different than you've been for a long time," William said as he led the way toward a grouping of future. "Why *do* you seem so refreshed, so… uplifted these days? I know my father's death affected you as well as it did me."

"That is true, I suppose, and it's a two-fold issue." Damn, how to broach the subject? "When your father died, I think, perhaps, these past two weeks have proved an epiphany of sorts. I want something permanent in my life, to leave a legacy as your father has."

Speculation reflected in William's eyes as he took another large sip of his brandy. "And all of that has made you think toward domesticity?"

"A bit."

Surprise etched through the other man's face. "Does that mean you've found a woman you wish to court for marriage?"

Did it? After spending the time with Diana, he rather thought he wanted her in all the ways that mattered. It had happened so swiftly and so quietly that he hadn't suspected that's what he was feeling—along with desire and pure lust, of course—but now that he knew what it was, it was rather… lovely. But he nodded. "Perhaps."

"Ah! Tell me." William tossed back the remainder of his drink then rested the empty glass on a nearby table.

"Uh…" Perhaps he should be vague until he could work out his thoughts. "Let us just say there is a possibility, an inkling of a dream of a woman I would like to take to wife." The idea of having Diana in his life exclusively cause his lips to curve with a grin. "Obviously, there are matters I'll need to work through, but I hope fate will let this come to fruition."

"I'm glad for you." William perched on the bolstered arm of a sofa. "Will you let me meet her?"

Well, shit.

That's when Nathaniel's courage gave out. Perhaps he wasn't ready to tell William that he wanted his older sister. "In time," he said in a graveled voice. "This is all new, and I don't wish to ruin it by talking about it prematurely."

"Fair enough." Yet William still regarded him with skepticism. "Does that mean you'll give up your rakish ways?"

"For this woman? I would do much merely to win her favor or see her smile." *Fuck me.* Had he admitted too much? Would William suspect? "She is quite different from anyone I've ever met." And what was more, all of what he'd said was true. He was ready… *if* that was what he ultimately wanted for his life. Not having children would prove an issue, though. Would that prove a sticking point?

Slowly, William nodded. "I'm impressed, old chap. Concerned about you being of sound mind, of course, but impressed. However, I will not follow in your stead, at least not right now."

Nathaniel allowed a grin as he collapsed into one of the delicate chairs. "Thank you. I'm looking forward to discovering what else I am capable of in this new realm." And he couldn't wait to see Diana at dinner tonight. He might not be able to give away his secret to the rest of the family or even have time alone with her, but it was better than nothing.

"Well, once Diana marries again, I'll be the only hold-out, which means Mama will turn her attention to finding me a match. A new countess will require someone with the right pedigree, but at least it will help her through the grieving process." He pulled a face. "I don't want that yet, of course, not with everything else, but I'll need an heir, and you and I are both getting up there in age."

"As if we're ancient bachelors…" Then the words sank into Nathaniel's brain. What had William just said? He frowned. "Did your sister mention something about marrying again?"

"Not in so many words, and she is dragging her feet, postponing things, for that was the sole reason she wished to go back into society. Papa's death will further delay it unless she wishes to have a quiet wedding." He shrugged. "However, I believe one of my friends will be the perfect husband for her, and what's more, he's a few years older than she, has a decent income, will treat her like a queen."

What sort of shit was this? The urge to be ill came over him. "Who is it?" He could barely spit out the words around his clenched teeth.

"The Marquess of Treverston. I met him at my club a couple of years ago. As I said, he's a decent chap, and I think he'll get on well with Diana."

"I know of him. He has three young children, all under eight, because his wife died suddenly a year or so ago. That's why he wishes to wed." In some agitation, Nathaniel stood. He slammed his brandy glass onto a table. Some of the remaining, amber-colored liquid jumped over the rim to splash onto the wood. "Diana has already raised her children and been a mother. She doesn't need to wed some man merely to do all of that again."

William huffed. "It's only a part of it."

"No." He shook his head as hot anger built in his chest.

"That's not fair to her. She should enjoy this time in her life, do things that make her happy. Frankly, your sister deserves every good thing. What she doesn't need is an elevated title with some nob who drinks more than is good for him and wants a new mother for his brood." Under no circumstances would he allow Diana to toss the remainder of her life away on something as unfulfilling as that.

"What the hell, Holdcraft?" William glared at him, looked as though Nathaniel had suddenly grown a second head. "Why fly into the boughs? It doesn't concern you. My sister is an acquaintance at the least and family at best."

"Exactly, which means I'm a bit protective of her, but neither does her life concern you. She can make her own choices." Though to be fair, an earl's daughter had more in common with a marquess than a viscount. "Isn't it time she does that for her own benefit? Have you even asked her what she wants?"

"Why do you care?" William stood and crossed his arms at his chest. "You're behaving as if you've gone mad."

Perhaps he had. "Someone has to protect her since her first marriage was rubbish. Where were you when that occurred?"

"In the military, you great nodcock. You knew that." Then he narrowed his eyes. "Did Diana tell you about her union?"

Heat sneaked up the back of his neck. "She did."

"When?"

"It doesn't matter." And he certainly would tell his best friend that he'd done unspeakable things to his older sister. "We *are* friends, after all."

"That makes no sense. Why the hell are you suddenly over-protective of her, a woman older than you? A woman you hadn't seen in over twenty years up until three weeks ago?"

And he definitely wasn't going to answer *that* question. "What does that matter?"

The other man shook his head. "I find it odd, is all."

"I am allowed to care for people other than you. Hell, I'm concerned over your mother's health just now, too. Will you come the crab about that, too?" When William said nothing, Nathaniel huffed. In danger of saying far too much and showing his hand prematurely, he shook his head. "If you will excuse me, I'm going to get some air."

"But I don't understand what upset you. The fact Diana might marry or the fact I won't?"

What the devil did that even mean? He blinked rapidly. Was that truly what William thought? He shook his head. "I'm not upset. I merely need to clear my head before I say something stupid, and now is not the time for you to pick a fight. Grief controls your thoughts and emotions right now. We can revisit this conversation at a later date."

"Fair enough." William glared. "Dinner will be called in half an hour. Don't go far."

How can I when I'm caught in Diana's gravitational pull?

"Of course I won't." Out of sorts with his best friend, Nathaniel stormed downstairs, passing Diana's son and daughter on the stairs. They both glanced at him with cheerful, welcoming expressions, and not wishing to stop and talk, he mumbled greetings, then he continued to the main level, pausing only when he reached the library.

Damnation.

Of course Diana was there, reading quietly in a shadowy corner. He almost didn't see her, dressed as she was in a black gown with glittering jet beads that lined the bodice. The silver in her hair almost sparkled in the dim illumination.

Immediately, he felt better. "You'll ruin your eyes. Come nearer to the candlelight," he said, as he came further into the room.

She glanced over at him with a ready smile. "I'm happy here, though."

"No doubt you are." With a glance to the door, he crept over the floor to her location. Because he needed to touch her, he silently, he took her hand and brought her swiftly to her feet, then he snuck an arm about her waist and claimed her lips in a kiss he'd been wanting since she left his carriage last night.

"Oh…" She fairly melted into his hold. The book fell to the carpet as she looped her arms around him and kissed him back with a low-grade hunger that he felt in his bones. Briefly, their tongues thrust and parried in a duel as old as time, but seconds later, she planted a palm on his chest and pushed him away. "As lovely as this interlude is, we should stop."

Heat and desire prowled through his insides. "Why?" All he wanted to do was lead her further into the shadows and have his wicked way with her.

Those highly kissable lips curved into a smile while amusement danced in her eyes. "Because we can easily be discovered, and I'm not of a mind to listen to a lecture from either William or my son." When he stared, she chuckled, and he would pay any amount of coin to hear that sound again. "Apparently, the men in my life believe I can't build my own future."

At least she would fight William's plans. "You don't think they know best?" Nathaniel stepped backward and put copious amounts of space between them, merely so he wouldn't be tempted by her.

"I do not. I want what I want, regardless of what they think."

Relief slid down his spine. "Uh, when can I see you again? And I don't mean at dinner," he whispered, as he edged to the middle of the room just to make certain that he wouldn't go back on his own word.

She met his gaze, and he swore he almost dove into those sapphire depths. "Call tomorrow afternoon. My son has an appointment out. My daughter is going shopping and visiting with her friends. That means I'll be free until dinner."

"I look forward to it." Then he winked because his heart felt all too light to know she wasn't going along with her brother's plans. "I need to go outside for some air. Which is what I told William to begin with."

"Why? It's raining."

"I'm aware of that, but becoming slightly damp is much better than going back to that drawing room with a cockstand." He snickered. "That is one conversation I refuse to have with your brother." Or even her son.

"Oh." When she giggled, she trailed her gaze down his body to rest briefly at the front of his evening breeches. "Too bad we are out of time."

"Indeed." Then, he fled the library to the soft sound of Diana's chuckle, which had his world tilting.

Shit, I've nearly tossed my hat over the windmill.

And it wasn't as bad as he'd feared. In fact, it left him quite… hopeful, and he hadn't had that in far too many years.

Chapter Thirteen

May 14, 1817
Atterbury House
Grosvenor Square
Mayfair, London

DIANA OPENED ONE of the windows in the drawing room, pushed it as far as it would go to encourage fresh air into the space. Remarkably, it wasn't raining, and the warmth of the sun on her face made her smile. If her cousin hadn't come to visit, she might have gone on a walk through Mayfair merely to take in the glorious weather.

As she turned about and looked at Tabetha, she said, "If you wish to go driving, I can call for the open carriage. We could enjoy the spring air and sunshine."

The other lady waved a hand from her perch on one of the delicate chairs in the room. "That's not necessary, for I won't be here long. I merely wished to pay a call and see how you fared following your father's death."

Though the ever-present sadness persisted, Diana nodded. She drifted close and sat in a matching chair. "Papa left a hole in my life, of course, but I am doing well enough. Trying to keep busy so I don't think about his loss so much." Yes, she was happy to spend time with her cousin, but her nerves were on edge, for Nathaniel would arrive soon. "How are you with your husband's health? Has there been any change?"

A sigh escaped Tabetha. "He's a bit better, but the doctor says the rally probably won't last." Shadows clouded her eyes. "It's odd, this waiting for the next phase of life while the current one is fading."

"I know exactly what you mean. That was how it was like with Papa's ailing health." To be fair, she would rather have that than be told unexpectedly of a loved one's death. "Honestly, why are you visiting me, then? Time is precious. You should be with him." As a ball of tears lodged in her throat, Diana swallowed it down. "If I've learned anything over the past two years, it's you can't avoid death. It will come for us all, eventually, so you need to make the most of the time with the people you love while you can."

Would she have wished to spend more time with her father? Of course, but life had a way of getting in the way of things, and sometimes good intentions were lost to the wind.

"I will." Tabetha nodded. She rested her gaze on Diana's face. "I wanted to see how you fared since we haven't talked in a bit." A sigh escaped her. "I'm sorry I didn't join the procession, but I couldn't leave London with my husband's health as it is."

"Oh, I know." Diana waved away her comment. "You were there in spirit. However, it was a lovely procession and service as he was laid to rest. Papa would have been pleased, I think." Despite the subject matter, she allowed a small grin as she again looked toward the doorway. "Family gathered around, and I was glad that Surrey was so close."

"Mmm." Then Tabetha peered more intently at her. Here eyebrows rose. "Why didn't you tell me that you have a man in your life?"

"What?" Knots of worry twisted in her stomach. Was it that obvious she'd entered into an affair? She laughed, but it sounded far too forced to her own ears. "That's silly." Heat slapped at her cheeks.

"Is it?" Her cousin smiled. A knowing look crossed her face. "Then tell me why you are distracted when you've never been that before, why you keep glancing at the door as if expecting someone? Oh, and just now, you blushed as if we were back in finishing school." A chuckle left her throat. "Who is it?"

"Um… uh…" What would it hurt to tell her cousin? Diana lowered her voice. "This stays between us."

"Of course." Tabetha leaned forward with expectation.

"It's Lord Holdcraft. We recently renewed our acquaintance and had a few… encounters before I had to go away for my father's funeral. I'm anxious to be alone with him again."

"What?" Her cousin gawked at her with a slightly open jaw. "But he's a known rake."

"Who hasn't been with a woman since we met."

"Perhaps, but he's younger than you."

Diana snorted. "Not by much. Only five years. It doesn't matter in the grand scheme."

"Oh, but it does. Rumor holds that he needs to marry for an heir." Tabetha frowned, as a look of concern went over her face. "Are you able to fall pregnant any longer?"

"Honestly, I don't know." More knots of worry pulled in her belly. Truth to tell, she hadn't had her menses for many months. In fact, she couldn't remember when the last time was, but she hadn't wondered since she'd been a widow for two years.

"Oh, Diana." Tabetha reached out and put a hand on hers. "Even if Lord Holdcraft has feelings for you, what you two are currently enjoying can't go into marriage. What good would it do for him?"

"I…" Blinking away the sudden tears in her eyes, she strove to hide her hurt feelings even though she'd had those same thoughts. "Well, there is only the physical between us, an affair if you will. We haven't spoken about anything else." And probably wouldn't.

Yet did she want more?

Tabetha sighed. "I don't think he's good enough for you anyway. You don't need a rake in your life."

She appreciated the distraction of that. "Yes, but there is a reason for that. He's been hurt deeply by women in the past and is guarding his heart by entering shallow relationships." Said aloud, it sounded poor. Perhaps she was a fool after all.

"Pish-posh." Her cousin waved a hand. "They all say that. Men don't change, and you of all women have cause to know that."

"They do if they have a good reason to do so." The urge to cry returned. As best she could, Diana squelched it. She strove for an attitude of no worries. "Put the concerns out of your mind. What is between Lord Holdcraft and me isn't that serious. We can walk away at any time."

In fact, how could it be serious when they hadn't had a chance to spend that much time together? Did it matter that the hours they'd had were deep and meaningful? That he'd made her feel so completely different from how Atterbury had done? That his kisses both set her ablaze but also made her feel young again and needed?

"Oh, goodness." Tabetha gasped as she stared at Diana. "Never say you've fallen in love him?" Shock wove through her voice.

Had she? "I... I don't know..." Surely that wasn't what some of the deeper feelings were, but they certainly went beyond the physical. How could it have happened in such a short time, though?

"Ha." Her cousin snorted. "I never figured you for a liar. What are you going to do?"

What indeed. Diana shrugged. "Let things continue as they are?" After all, she couldn't marry him because he needed an heir. The best she could do was be his mistress, but how could she stand by and watch him marry someone else? Give his body, his heart, his soul to another woman, one who would bear his children, one who would reap the benefits of being a family with him?

Good heavens, that would prove more devastating than being ignored in her own marriage. Tears welled in her eyes, and she couldn't blink them away quickly enough. When they fell to her cheeks, she brushed them from her skin. Why was life so cruel?

The arrival of the butler prevented the conversation from moving forward. Thank goodness.

"Pardon the interruption, my lady, but Lord Holdcraft is here. Are you receiving?"

Her traitorous heart leapt at the news, and she gasped. With heat burning through her cheeks, Diana said, "Please send him up."

Once the butler left, Tabetha grinned as she stood. "Not in love, eh?" she said in a soft voice. "I rather think you're lying."

She ignored the observation. "Are you leaving?"

"I am, for I'm quite certain my presence will soon be *de trop*." With a wink, she shook the wrinkles from her skirting. "Besides, I'm going home to my husband. You've reminded me of what love feels like. I want to feel that for as long as I can with mine." Tabetha lowered her voice. "But I expect you to tell me everything later."

Seconds later, her cousin exited the room. The sound of polite greetings from the corridor told Diana that the viscount was talking with her cousin. His deep cadence coupled with Tabetha's high, thin tone made her grin.

Then he came into the room with a flat rectangle box in his hand. "Good afternoon, Lady Diana," he said with a wink. "Was that your cousin?"

"Yes." Slowly, she gained her feet. "Tabetha came by to see how I fared, but her husband is ailing. She wanted to go home and spend time with him, which was why you met her in the corridor."

"Ah." He nodded. "It seems everyone is struggling these days." Once he'd closed the distance between them, the viscount offered her the box. "This is for you. A gift."

Frissons of excitement twisted down her spine. When was the last time she'd been given anything from a man, aside from the flowers he'd offered twice before? "Why?"

"Well, May Day came and went during a sad time, so I didn't have a chance to ply you with mysterious tokens of my affection, or to even give you flowers." The look in his eyes promised wicked things. "I'm making up for it now."

"What a lovely gesture." When she opened the blue linen-covered box, a gasp left her throat. "Good heavens, Nathaniel. They're beautiful!" Inside was a long rope of perfectly matched pearls that gleamed in the sunlight, tied in two loops by a black satin ribbon. "It's far too much." And since the box was new and had the name of a prominent London jeweler in foiled silver lettering on the inside of the lid, he must have recently bought it, which meant she'd been on his mind. Heat went through her cheeks. "Far too much," she reiterated in a whisper even as she caressed a fingertip over the jewels from the sea.

"Nonsense. Every lady needs pearls, and the ribbon is for your hair during this trying time." He met her gaze with somber understanding. "I hope you'll wear them even if you can't attend society events just now."

Was there anyone as dear as this man? "I will." Suddenly, she made a decision, and reminding herself that she was a widow with some level of freedom in society, she took his hand with her free one. "In fact, come with me."

"Why?" His sensual lips turned down in a frown. "Where are we going?"

Her heartbeat accelerated. "To my rooms. We only have a bit of time and can't waste it." Feeling quite naughty and far too scandalous, Diana led him from the room then glanced at him from over her shoulder. "I've missed being with you. Frankly, I won't be satisfied until we're both naked and in my bed." She was beyond caring if that made her sound desperate, but she *was* haunted by the conversation she'd just had with her cousin.

Finding release with the viscount would go a long way into consoling her.

"Who am I to argue with a beautiful lady?" Amusement threaded through his voice.

"You are a quick study, Holdcraft. That will serve you well." Once in her rooms, she softly closed the corridor door and locked it then she did the same with the door to the adjoining dressing room. When she joined him again, she raked her gaze up and down his form. "Take your clothes off."

Surprise jumped into his expression. His eyes rounded. "What?"

It was rather interesting to assume the power in this carnal session. "You heard me. Take off your clothes. I'll do the same. I don't want barriers or delays when I launch my seduction."

"This forceful side of you is damned arousing," he said as he reached for the folds of his cravat.

In silence, they both disrobed, and once she hadn't a stitch of clothing on, Diana donned the strand of pearls, which she looped around her neck twice. She left the ribbon and the box on the top of her bureau.

"How do they look?" she asked in a low voice she hoped he found seductive. Of course, she couldn't help but admire his naked form and his erect member. It was quite flattering to know that she could inspire him in that way even with her own body with its share of skin that slightly sagged with age, her breasts that weren't as perky as they'd once been, and marks and scars on her body from childbirth and the simple act of living.

"As tempting as always," he responded, though his gaze was very clearly on her breasts and the tightening nipples. A chuckle left him. "Ah, but you meant the pearls." He came closer, touched a fingertip to one of the coils. "As gorgeous as the woman who wears them."

"Such a charmer." His words encased her in a cocoon of heat and safety. "But I don't want conversation; I merely want you." Maneuvering him over the floor, she then pushed him into a comfortable, brocade, wingback chair near the window and climbed into his lap, straddling him. "Is that acceptable?"

"It sure as hell is." Seconds later, he slipped a hand around her nape, drew her to him, and kissed her with intent and a certain hardness whose sole purpose was to stake his claim and show his possessiveness.

Though she didn't mind that statement, she wished to make one of her own. Moving into a more comfortable position on his lap with his thick shaft rubbing the curve of her arse, Diana took command of the embrace. It was her who chased his tongue and her who thrust and parried with it first until he was fully engaged. When she flicked a fingernail over one of his erect nipples and he sucked in a breath, she grinned and didn't let up with her torture.

"Turnabout is fair play," Nathaniel whispered against her lips right before he dragged his lips down the side of her neck.

"Do your worst, Holdcraft." Oh, this man's attentions revitalized her, reminded her that she wasn't too old nor that her usefulness was over in a society that told her in many ways each day that she was.

"Or rather my best." His hands were on her breasts, holding them, mashing them together, squeezing them in a dizzying array of movements designed to build excitement and anticipation. When he rolled her nipples, gently plucked and pinched them to prolong a cycle of pain and pleasure, she couldn't help the moan that escaped her.

Moments later, hands and fingers were everywhere, chased by lips and tongues on heated skin and sensitive body parts. She was in danger of being lost in him, but then, his body was quite delicious, and it couldn't be helped.

The more she explored and kissed him, the greater the molten need within built. When she couldn't bear the terrible pressure stacking low in her belly a second longer, Diana rose onto her knees. She took his thick, hot length in her hand and guided the head of his member to her opening. As she held his gaze, ran the risk of tumbling into those mossy depths, she slowly impaled herself onto his hard shaft. That moment of initial penetration was so lovely that she shivered with the sheer joy of it then lifted off him.

With questions in his eyes, he gripped her hips while she

rested her hands on his shoulders, then with a nod, he flexed his hips and thrust upward at the same time she crashed down onto him again. The resulting crash left them both gasping.

There was no need for words; they both knew what they wanted from each other.

Each time he thrust upward, she met those strokes by bobbing down. Easily, they found a rhythm, but penetration went deep, so impossibly deep in this position. Almost immediately, urgency guided her movements. As she slipped more frantically along his shaft, the need for release grew and expanded within her. Concentration lay etched over his face as he fought with his own needs and against the want to spend.

Yet it was only a matter of time before they both broke.

Diana gyrated her hips, guided by his hold on her, worked herself back and forth over his thrusting shaft. The dam within splintered apart before she was ready. The swirling vortex of bliss rushed up to engulf her into its pull. Contractions racked her body. A soft cry left her throat, but the viscount quickly claimed her lips, taking the sound into himself. After another hard push, he followed her into pleasure, but she ground her pelvis against his in an effort to prolong all those lovely sensations.

Eventually, their bodies ceased to move together. She collapsed into his chest. Nathaniel wrapped his arms around her. The ragged sound of their breathing echoed in the silence. The tactile feel of him, the way the coarse hair on his chest bedeviled her overly sensitive nipples sent tiny shivers of residual delight down her spine. The way his shaft still twitched as it stayed embedded in her body reminded her of the trust she had in him by sharing the greatest intimacy she'd just shared with him. Never would she grow used to this act and how with Nathaniel, she was free to be herself, free of judgment or properness, and she could chase pleasure however she wanted.

Remaining in his hold as they both came back to Earth was such a precious boon and one she never had with Atterbury. She might enjoy it as much as the sex act, and that was enough to boggle her mind. Eventually, Diana stirred against him.

With a lingering kiss to his lips, she pulled slightly away. "My daughter will be home soon. You must go." Though, it would have been quite a lovely afternoon if he could stay and spend time with her involved in mundane domestic tasks.

"Damn, this interlude went by far too quickly." But he nodded and brushed his lips over hers. "Thank you for this afternoon. I can't remember when I last enjoyed myself this much." A twinkle set up in his eyes that made her want to toss him to the bed and have at him all over again. "Also, you *are* gorgeous in the pearls, but then, I thought that before you donned them."

"Do stop. Such gammon." But heat filled her cheeks all the same.

"The truth." He dropped a gentle kiss on her lips before helping her off his lap. "When can I see you again?" A few moments went by while he gathered his clothing from the floor. "I rather think I'm becoming addicted to you."

"Oh!" Her heart trembled. "Perhaps tomorrow afternoon?"

The viscount yanked his lawn shirt over his head. As he thrust his arms into the sleeves and tugged the garment down over his chest, he asked, "Here?"

"Yes." Diana donned her abandoned chemise. "If the day is fine, perhaps we can go driving."

"Then let us hope fate conspires in our favor." When he winked, her heartbeat accelerated. "And wear the pearls. They've given me ideas."

Too much more of that, and she wouldn't be able to survive him, but she smiled.

After he left, she donned a lace-edged wrap then collapsed on her bed. "What am I going to do now?" Somehow, she'd fallen in love with him, yet in her heart of hearts, she knew she'd have to break his, because she simply wasn't what he needed.

CHAPTER FOURTEEN

May 15, 1817
Atterbury House
Grosvenor Square
Mayfair, London

NATHANIEL GRINNED TO himself. Earlier in the afternoon, he'd taken Diana driving through Hyde Park. It had been splendid, and oddly enough, he'd never taken any other woman driving or on any sort of outing. Not since the last one he thought he'd marry. But there was something compelling and special about Diana, and he wanted to experience everything with her, for it all felt new to him in her company.

However, because she was scheduled to accompany her daughter on an errand later in the afternoon, his time with her was limited.

That suited his own needs just fine, for Nathaniel was determined to snap her up and secure their future before her brother ruined everything with shoving her into the marquess's path. When he was shown into the house, he asked to speak with Viscount Atterbury, and the butler eyed him askance for a quick second before showing him up to the drawing room.

Not long after, Percy joined him.

"What a surprise, Lord Holdcraft. I rarely have callers of any sort, let alone one of your caliber, but if you wish to see my mother, unfortunately, she is out."

"I actually came to see you."

The young viscount gestured toward a grouping of furniture, then proceeded to sit in a chair near the fireplace that remained dormant even though there was a bit of a spring chill in the air. "Why is that?"

Nathaniel sank into a matching chair, then half turned to face the other man. "We'll get to that in a moment, but first, how are you faring with the death of your grandfather?"

"Oh." Atterbury shrugged. "I'm doing well enough. Unfortunately, I didn't spend much time with him while I was away at school, and then with my father whenever he was hunting."

Right, and that was how he'd found his father, dead during one of those hunts. He nodded. "It seems the older one grows, the more difficult dividing one's time can be." While he indulged in small talk, he hoped his courage would bubble to the surface.

"Indeed. I have one year left at university, and where I thought to become a solicitor eventually, I've now been handed the reins of a viscounty." He shook his head with a frown. "Is it bad to admit that I'm not certain I wish to be that?"

"Not at all. Most of us have had such thoughts at one time or another." Truly, Percy was still young yet and had much maturing to do.

God, does that mean I have done the same since Diana came back into my life?

The other man heaved a sigh. "I don't know the direction I wish to take the title. Hell, I barely know anything about the estate." A hint of ruddy color slid up his neck above his cravat and collar. "To be honest, I have no clue or guidance on where to start."

"I remember that feeling." Nathaniel rested a leg on a knee. "However, I'm certain your father had a solicitor and a man-of-affairs. Call a meeting with them both. If you find you don't get on with either, you can let them go and hire your own." That in itself was a large task. "Also, if you'd like, I can help you with all of these things as well as talk about what you want for your estate and your future." He wished he'd had that when handed his own title.

"That is fantastic. Thank you." The young man nodded with enthusiasm. "So helpful, for I don't know where to start and I don't want to disappoint my mother."

Poor boy. He was already under a lot of strain. "I rather doubt that will happen. She dotes on you and your sister."

Surprise jumped into the viscount's eyes. "Mama told you about us?"

"She has talked to me on and off about the two of you, for she loves you to distraction. To be honest, I would like to learn more about you." He cleared his throat, for the time had come to broach the point of the visit. "In fact, that is one of the reasons I wished to talk with you today."

"Oh?"

Nathaniel nodded. "As you probably already know, your mother and I were acquaintances long ago, before she married your father. Our fathers' properties in Surrey border each other, so we grew up together." What else to say that would give him some background that might explain why he got on extremely well with Diana so quickly? "When I was a young man a couple of years younger than you, I carried a *tendre* for her, thought myself in love with her, but since my best friend is your uncle, he forbade me from any of that. And she was engaged to your father besides."

Too long-winded, Holdcraft. Do better.

"I might have heard something about how you all grew up, but why are you telling me this?" Confusion reflected in his eyes.

"Well, I needed to give you some context before this next bit."

"Very well."

He took a deep breath and let it ease out to calm his nerves. Never had he wanted anything more than opening the door to a possible future with Diana. "I hadn't thought about your mother, hadn't seen her during all the years of her marriage because I had my own interests. During that time my parents died, and I was handed the reins to my own viscounty." He shrugged. It was difficult putting so much history into a few minutes of talking. "I hadn't been aware she was a widow until recently."

Atterbury's gaze never left his face. "What happened?"

"Well, we came back into each other's lives unexpectedly. And there is a connection between us, a bond that has only strengthened as time goes on, which we discovered over the course of the past few weeks or so."

A snicker came from the younger man. "What are you trying to tell me, Lord Holdcraft? Best to just get it out."

"Right." Nathaniel nodded. "The truth is, I suspect that I am in love with your mother." There, he'd finally said it out loud, and he rather enjoyed saying it.

The viscount's eyebrow rose into his hair line. "Oh?"

"Indeed." He offered a grin that felt more relieved than happy. "In fact, there isn't anything I wouldn't do for her. I live to make her smile or hear her laugh. I want to look after her for the rest of my life, protect her from the ills in the world. She challenges me to be a better man. In her I've found hope again, and I want to build a life with her." That was the gist of it, truly. "In short, I'm asking for your permission to marry her."

"What?" The younger man stared at him with shock and surprise warring for dominance in his expression. "You love my mother." It wasn't a question.

"I do. Quite desperately, in fact, and I fear I've wasted enough time already, so I'd rather not put off the next steps if at all possible." Was he desperate or simply excited?

"Uh, Lord Holdcraft, you don't need *my* permission. If you wish to ask my mother to marry you, then do so."

Was the answer to the question that simple, then? "Perhaps, but you *are* her son, and as such, you are the head of the house. I also wanted to make certain you had no issues with me before I plead my case with her. If fate is kind and she accepts, I'd like for us to be a family without easily fixable issues up front."

God, how long had he wished for a family of his own without realizing it?

"While that makes sense, you should talk to my uncle, especially since he's your best friend. He's her brother and an earl now. Wouldn't he be the best one to speak to about this?"

Which was what he was trying to avoid. "Firstly, William doesn't think I'm good enough for your mother."

The other man's expression fell. "Oh."

Nathaniel nodded. "And secondly, I'd rather not poke a stick at that particular bear until I can secure your mother's hand. Then I thought we'd face him together. Otherwise, he wants her to marry a marquess who I know won't treat her as well as I can."

Damn, I probably shouldn't have said so much.

Silence reigned between them for longer than Nathaniel was comfortable with. As he opened his mouth to say something—anything—into the void, Atterbury interrupted.

"Because I'm curious, tell me *why* you like my mother."

Now that was a direct question that would consolidate everything else. "I appreciate the opportunity to delve deeper into that." He paused as he tried to organize his thoughts. "There is something about your mother—Diana—that has thrown my life topsy-turvy." And it was more than the white-hot carnal sessions they shared. "I could spend hours lost in her eyes. The sound of her voice is soothing. I've told her about my past, and she hasn't judged me for it." He shrugged, for he could spend days cataloguing why he adored her. "In short, she is unlike anyone else I've ever met." Merely thinking about her made him happy, and a grin skated over his face without him knowing it. When was the last time he'd truly been happy and ready to take on the day? "She just makes everything… better."

Atterbury regarded him with a goofy grin of his own. "It doesn't bother you that she's older than you?"

"Of course not." How did he know that? "Why should it? Age is merely a number, and we are good together. I'd like to discover more of what we can do as a couple." Then he frowned. Did the questions mean her son would ultimately refuse the match? "If you're wondering whether I can take care of her in a manner to which she's become accustomed, I can. I have a decent income from my estate and investments. I'm always looking to add more revenue streams and now is a good time for that. The world is constantly changing and growing. That means more opportunities will be available for men with coin to make a lot more of it. Hell, investing in steel is a good idea. I have a feeling this will prove invaluable to England soon."

"Good to know." Percy resettled himself in the chair as he met Nathaniel's gaze. "May I be truthful with you?"

"Of course." Cold trepidation coiled through his gut.

"Mama told Eliza and me about you a couple of days ago."

"Oh?" What the devil did that entail?

The younger man nodded. "We were catching up on each other's lives. When Eliza mentioned that Mama seemed happier, lighter than the last time we saw her, Mama admitted that she'd met a man who let her be herself and in the process had helped set her soul free so that she might fly. I didn't know what that meant at the time, but perhaps I do now you've said what you have."

"I see." What had happened to his words? Why couldn't he come up with something more erudite instead?

Young Atterbury continued. "What's more, there was life and interest and a new softness in her expression that day I hadn't seen during the course of my whole life." A mix of confusion once more took possession of his expression. "While I don't know what sort of man Papa was to her, I do know that she wasn't happy most of the time. To my way of thinking, a husband should make certain the woman he's wed to is at least that. Why else would he say vows to her?"

Ah, Percy was young yet and had much to learn about the world, but Nathaniel appreciated the sentiment. He cleared his throat. "There were some issues in that union, and she was deeply hurt from some of them, but they aren't my stories to tell." Not once did he drop his gaze. "You have my word I won't treat her like your father did. I only want what's best for her, to see her succeed, to give her love and space and understanding so she can continue to grow… exactly what she does for me."

"I rather think my mother is quite fortunate to have met you, Lord Holdcraft."

"While I appreciate that, it is beyond nerve-wracking to come here and talk about such things with you, so if you don't mind, could you either put me out of my misery or tell me to take my leave." Realizing that was rude, he held up a hand. "I apologize. I didn't mean it to sound like that."

Remarkably, the young man chuckled. "If that is what love does to a man your age, then I want no part of it any time soon. I value having a clear head." Then he grinned. "I can see how genuine you are about my mother, and I'm fairly confident she feels the same about you. In this, I'm glad she has you, because I also believe she deserves every good thing in life." Slowly, Atterbury rose to his feet. Nathaniel scrambled to his as well. "All of that being said, I give you my blessing. You may ask her to marry you."

"Truly?"

"Yes, truly." The younger man nodded. "I agree with you that Mama should go into this next phase of life with all the happiness the world can grant, and if she's found that with you, I'd be a nodcock to throw a stick in that wheel." He held out a hand. "Also, I feel that in the absence of my own father, you will prove an asset for me and my future, perhaps can help guide me in the direction I need to go so I don't muck up my own title."

"Thank you, and of course I'll mentor you." With nothing left to do, Nathaniel shook the offered hand. "In fact, I'd be honored to do exactly that." Then he frowned. "Should I speak with your sister before asking your mother for a private word?"

"Ha!" The viscount snorted. "Eliza will be over the moon. She still has stars in her eyes and believes in love and romance, which is how all those young women are in finishing school. I'm afraid life will change their minds soon enough."

In that, he had the air of a wizened little man.

"Besides, my sister will be thrilled that she'll have the excuse to order a new pretty gown and all the fripperies."

Nathaniel couldn't help his own chuckle. "That sounds far too true." He exchanged an exasperated glance with the younger man. "I shall call upon your mother this evening." No sense in delaying things now that he'd made his decision.

"Good man." The viscount led him across the room to the door. "I look forward to formally welcoming you into the family."

Family.

Moisture rose to his eyes as his chest tightened. He hadn't been part of a family for a very long time indeed, and now he was on the precipice of having just that. What was more, William would be his true brother, by marriage.

Tamping down on the emotions, Nathaniel paused in the corridor. "Thank you for your time. Now I need to procure a ring. You wouldn't happen to know what styles your mother prefers, would you?" Yes, he'd already given her the pearls, and they'd looked fantastic on her, but he wanted something more expensive to grace her finger.

"I'm afraid I don't pay that much attention, but I'm sure she'll adore whatever you choose."

With a nod, Nathaniel left the house.

Chapter Fifteen

Later that evening
Sammerson House
St. James's Place
Mayfair, London

DIANA HUMMED TO herself as she made her way upstairs to the drawing room of her parents' townhouse. No doubt William would move into it within weeks from his modest townhouse across Mayfair. After all, this building had been the home of the Earls of Northfield since their grandfather had been alive.

But that was an issue for another day. Tonight, she would take dinner with her family, and was content to do so, for suddenly everything in her life felt… magical.

All because of Nathaniel.

It was odd, this being hopeful in life, feeling as if her feet rarely touched the ground. She'd only known him for just over three weeks but hadn't even spent some of that time with him. However, the time she did have with him had been like lifetimes, and the connection between them had only strengthened.

Interesting how two men could affect her so differently. Where Atterbury had placed her firmly in second place behind his mistress and treated her as an afterthought, Nathaniel put her front and center in his life. He would do anything for her, would fetch the moon for her if she asked, and they were night and day opposites from each other.

In him, because of him, she'd found an inner strength she hadn't known she possessed, and thanks to him, she had learned that she was valued for who she was alone. He'd swept away the cobwebs from her soul and had given her a new outlook in all aspects of her life.

There was such freedom in the knowledge.

Now, as she and her family gathered in the drawing room ahead of dinner, she wondered how life would change again. How long would her affair with Nathaniel last? Eliza was scheduled to return to her finishing school to complete the last term of the year since her time away for mourning was at an end. Would Percy return to the Surrey property, or would he finally feel comfortable settling into London? She'd need to ask. However, if he *did* move permanently into her townhouse—which had belonged to his father in any event—her relationship with Nathaniel would need to be even more discreet.

To be fair, she didn't take issue in being at his home more than hers, but it would have been easier not to need plan heavily merely to be with him. But that was a part of life at times. The way things were, she was headed for dowager territory, and would definitely be that once Percy took a bride. Dear heavens, she hoped that wouldn't be for a few years yet since he was still in university, but that was a good thing. He would be away from London out of necessity due to schooling, so a sudden upheaval probably wouldn't occur soon.

Just thinking of the possibilities in the offing with Nathaniel made her both happy but sad, for she knew she ultimately wasn't the woman he needed in his life for the long term.

For now, she would enjoy him at whatever capacity he would give her.

When she entered the drawing room, she smiled at the people she loved best in the world. Everyone was there, with the exception of her sister and her sister's family. Going over to her mother, she bussed her parent's cheek.

"Perhaps this isn't the time, but that black crepe is becoming on you, Mama." The gown was simple in lines and designs, but she had accepted the shoulders and bodice with a dark-gray tulle.

Her mother inclined her head with a faint smile. "Thank you, and I'm glad you wore the lavender. It's not fair to plunge you back in mourning when you've barely gotten out of it."

"Oh, I just haven't had time to select gowns for dyeing." But she was secretly pleased because her gown was a favorite.

Made of a lavender silk blend, it featured soft ivory lace around the bodice and the slightly off-the-shoulder neckline. As a concession to her father's death, she'd tied a black satin sash about her waist. Though it featured long sleeves, they were quite thin and had been gathered in increments reminiscent of a medieval style. Matching lace lined the edge of the sleeve at her wrist. Since it was still spring and she was in such an uplifted mood, she'd pinned small silk daisies into her loose chignon. Around her neck, she wore the rope of pearls Nathaniel had given her. The two loops sat cool against her skin, and with every brush of her fingertips, she remembered what he'd said when he gave her the necklace and that coupling they'd indulged in directly afterward.

Her mother shook her head. "Lavender is still acceptable for mourning, and we're staying in, so it doesn't fully matter."

William nodded. "You are quite striking tonight, Sis. Good show. Quite fitting of your age and status."

"My age?"

He coughed. "What I meant was that all too often, women try to wear styles that don't suit them. But then, you have always had a tasteful way of dressing."

While her children snickered, and before Diana could respond, someone else entered the drawing room, and when she lifted her head to see why her daughter was suddenly quite excited, her own heart skipped a beat.

"Nathaniel," she said in a choked whisper. "Er, I mean, Lord Holdcraft. Welcome." She'd had no idea he would attend dinner with them tonight.

"Good evening, Lady Diana," he said with a wink as he strode into the space, full of the confidence and self-assurance that she so admired.

Oh, but he was so handsome tonight! No matter that there were others in the room, she roved her gaze up and down his person. Red hair arranged into a popular style, his collar points just so, and the snowy folds of his cravat precisely set, he was every inch a gentleman about Town. The jacket of sapphire superfine hugged his broad shoulders and chest to perfection, and the silver waistcoat she'd seen on him before highlighted how lean he was beneath the clothing. The black breeches and recently shined boots set off his powerful legs that were like a dream, and she particularly liked that he hadn't worn the requisite evening clothing.

I do admire a man willing to defy social traditions upon occasion.

Then he was before her, taking her hand and bringing it to his lips. "You are easily the most beautiful woman in Mayfair tonight," he said in a whisper, before kissing the back of her hand.

"Thank you." There was a certain light in his eyes and a soft curve to his lips that had her trembling with need. Too bad dinner would be called soon, for she would have liked to pull him aside and kiss him for a few moments.

"Holdcraft!" William's greeting boomed through the room from the direction of the sideboard, and the surprise on his face was genuine. Clearly, he hadn't expected his best friend. "I'm glad to see you. Do you join us for dinner?"

Nathaniel glanced his way. "If you'll have me." Then, with a wink at Diana, he crossed the room to where her mother sat on a sofa, took her hand, and then kissed the back, much to her mother's amusement. Her giggle was unexpected. Afterward, he gave Eliza's hand the same treatment, and as her daughter simpered and blushed, Diana's heart squeezed.

Dear heavens, he is quite a rogue. She fanned her face with a hand as heat crept into her own cheeks.

"Of course!" William grinned as he brought over a cut-crystal glass of brandy for his friend. "You are always welcome here." When he pressed the vessel into Nathaniel's hand, he peered into his face. "You have the look of a changed man. What has occurred since the last time we spoke? You seem as if you've had an epiphany."

Diana glanced at him as she sank into a chair nearby. He did, indeed, have an air of one who has a jolly secret.

"Ha! I *have* wrestled with some thoughts in my mind, but because of this, I have come to a decision." With a glance at her son, who gave him a small nod, Nathaniel grinned. He moved over the floor to sit in the chair beside hers. He rested his glass on the low table in front of them. "And that decision has brought me to you, Lady Diana."

"Me?" Her heartbeat accelerated as she met his gaze. "Why?" What was happening?

"It's true." He nodded as if she might misunderstand him. "It's fitting that I'll ask this of you while in the midst of your family, for I have long felt a part of it as well, and in lieu of my own, I've been quite at home here, and welcomed as well."

None of it made sense, but flutters went through her lower belly all the same. And why was Percy looking on with anticipation in his expression? "What are you going on about?"

"Yes, Holdcraft, you're acting quite odd," William said, then took a sip of his brandy.

"Perhaps I am, but there's a reason for that." With secrets and emotions in his eyes, Nathaniel took her hand. "Diana, I never thought I would find myself feeling the way I do for you now. In fact, I've always thought I would remain alone for a good portion of my life. Yet you came back into my life and caught me by surprise with all the force as if you landed me a facer."

"Oh, goodness…" Her whispered words faded away on the heels of a gasp.

"What is this, then? *She's* the woman you told me about?" William asked, but their mother told him to hush.

Nathaniel nodded. "I can save a longer speech for when we're alone, but suffice it to say, I have unexpectedly fallen in love with you. If you can see your way toward a future today, will you make me the happiest of men by marrying me?"

A girlish sigh from Eliza punctuated the silence that followed the question.

Before Diana could answer, William loudly objected.

"Absolutely not!" Her brother strode over to yank Nathaniel from his chair as he glared at him. "Our friendship notwithstanding, there are far too many reasons why I will not allow my sister—my *older* sister—to marry you."

"What the hell is wrong with me?" Nathaniel demanded with an expression reminiscent of a summer thunderstorm.

"If you don't know, you're a bigger nodcock than I assumed." William poked him in the chest with a forefinger. "Firstly, you're younger than her. Second, you're a damned rake who I rather doubt could remain loyal to one woman for more than an hour. And third, don't you think I know more about who the better man for her is than you since I've known her my whole life, whereas you have a twenty-two-year gap in your history?"

"Pardon my language, ladies, but fuck off, William." He shoved against her brother's chest, and William stumbled backward. "You know nothing about what is happening here."

Percy, God bless him, shot to his feet. "Uh, Uncle William, perhaps you should hear him out before you do something…"

With a growl, William drew back a fist and landed a punch that caught Nathaniel in the chin, sending him crashing to the floor, narrowly missing the edge of the table with his head.

"…rash," Percy finished in an ironic voice.

"Enough of this." The viscount picked himself off the floor and ignored her brother in order to concentrate on Diana, who'd jumped to her feet the moment he'd fallen. "Please listen." He dropped to one knee and took her hand. The red mark on his left cheek where William had punched him looked rather angry.

"I don't think—"

"Please." He implored her with his gaze, and she was powerless against the pleading in those mossy depths. "Despite your brother's objection, I wish to persist because... because I love you, Diana. Marry me. Spend the remainder of your life with me and let me spend the rest of mine showing you how you should have been treated all along; You deserve every good thing, and frankly, you are simply wonderful."

Heavy silence reigned in the room as everyone stared at them. Eliza had a hand to her mouth, and her eyes were round and wide with excitement, while Percy looked on with mixed feelings on his face.

How embarrassing and somewhat overwhelming.

"Oh, Nathaniel." Heat seeped into Diana's cheeks as she clutched at his hand. "These past weeks with you have been lovely, beyond my wildest dreams, really."

"Weeks?" William interrupted yet again with another glare at her. "You've been seeing him for *weeks*?"

They both ignored him.

Diana pressed her lips together as the urge to cast up her accounts grew strong in her chest, for she knew what her next words would do to him in light of his previous bad luck in love and romance. "Truly, you are an amazing man, a good man, and seeing a change in you makes my heart soar, but I am sorry. I really am." Her chin trembled and tears welled in her eyes. "However, I cannot, in good conscience, marry you. It wouldn't be right."

Gasps punctuated the silence, coming from the dowager and Eliza. Even her son looked shocked and perplexed.

"What?" The whispered inquiry from him sounded overly loud in the space. The crestfallen expression on Nathaniel's face felt like a dagger to her heart. "Why? I thought we might have had a connection, the same hope..."

Quickly, she shook her head. "It doesn't matter, but my answer is no, and it's quite final." Then because she couldn't bear to be the center of attention or to see the various expressions of confusion and disappointment on the faces around her, Diana ran from the room.

Oh, why couldn't he leave well enough alone? Why couldn't they both have been content with a mere affair?

Atterbury House
Grosvenor Square
Mayfair, London

IT HAD BEEN an hour since she'd run from the drawing room at her brother's home. An hour since she'd rejected Nathaniel's proposal. An hour since her heart had broken into a million pieces because she'd shattered his. It mattered not what she wanted for herself or for her future, because she was doing him a favor even if he couldn't see that yet.

At some point, he would thank her, if only as a memory.

The only thing to do now was hide in her suite and let regret have at her. Would she even have the wherewithal to concentrate on reading a book? She didn't know, but she made her way to her sitting room, where she promptly threw herself down onto a low sofa upholstered in crushed velvet and let herself cry out her feelings. When her maid came in, concerned, she dismissed her, saying firmly that she wouldn't require assistance until the morning.

Barely an hour after that, the sound of angry footsteps moving swiftly along the corridor reached her ears. By the time Diana had struggled into a sitting position, the door flew open and Nathaniel stood in the frame. He'd tracked her down, for of course he had, and as much as she didn't want to have this conversation, it couldn't be postponed.

Wiping at the moisture on her cheeks, she shook her head, wishing she felt dead inside instead of this jumble of emotions. "Go away, Nathaniel." She sniffled into a handkerchief as she stood. "I don't want to talk."

"I'm not going anywhere until you explain to me why you rejected my suit." Anger shadowed his eyes. "You left me in that drawing room confused and embarrassed. Then I was forced to have yet another shouting match with your damned brother. I'd rather not spend another hour trying to explain myself to him."

Despite herself, she was curious. "What happened?"

He shrugged. There was no trace of humor or charm left on his face. "I finally landed him a facer merely to shut him up, told him that both you and I were capable of guiding our own futures, and then I left. For a long time I sat in my carriage wondering what to do, but damn it, I'm not giving up on us."

"Oh." Drat it all. Why did her heart have to skip like that? "I said what I did *for* you."

A huff escaped him. "You'll have to try again because that makes no sense."

She nodded. "I'm older than you, and I didn't realize it until too late that I probably am past the age where I can bear children. Since you need an heir, I decided to cut you loose before too much damage had been done." It sounded cold to her ears, but there was nothing for it.

"Such gammon, Diana, and you know it." Annoyance rumbled in his voice. "Did it ever occur to you that I might not care about any of that? That I might just want you?"

"That's careless. You have responsibilities to your title." She tried moving into the adjoining bedroom to get away from him, but he was having none of it.

He made a crude gesture that both shocked and intrigued her. "The title can go fallow for all I care. Let parliament unknot the tangles." Without another word, he followed her into the bed chamber, then slammed the door to the dressing room, and threw the locking mechanism.

Awareness of him prickled along her skin. "What are you doing?"

"Making a more convincing argument. If you don't believe

my words, perhaps you'll believe what my body tells you, what yours says when it responds." He pounced, and during a series of searing kisses no doubt designed to punish for or object to what she'd said earlier, clothes were angrily removed until they were once more naked together in her bedroom. Clearly, he was a man bent on seduction.

Or retribution.

"Nathaniel, I don't think…"

"Too much thinking is often the problem. It certainly has been just now." He plundered her mouth with a string of deep, drugging kisses while the other hand went to her breast and quickly brought the nipple erect. Then he rolled that tip until she was gasping for breath, drowning in a myriad of sensations she couldn't quite keep ahead of. When he wrenched away, he said, "Afterward, we'll puzzle out how to go forward, but for now, this is what we'll say to each other."

Desire clouded her mind; pain shrouded her heart. The only reason she allowed the intrusion was because this would be her last time carnally with him. Such a thought brought tears to her eyes. Even the affair couldn't withstand the rejection she'd just handed him.

Nothing could, but his hands at her breasts and his lips at the side of her neck were quite distracting… from everything.

"Dear lord, you must leave off," she gasped out, for if he didn't, she would surely dissolve into a melted puddle on the floor.

"You were the one who declined my suit, who tore my world apart, so because I can't find the words to convince you, I'll send you flying instead," he said as he dropped to his knees and seconds later, he encouraged her legs apart. "I will say that you broke my heart, Diana, after everything." When his voice wavered, pain squeezed around *her* heart once more.

"I'm sorry, but you must know, when you're thinking clearly, that a future between us is ill-advised."

"Don't try to downplay or forget what we are to each other."

The dratted man glided his fingers along her flesh made slick from his teasing of her breasts, back and forth in a mesmerizing rhythm. Before she could utter a response, he'd coaxed her swelling nubbin out of hiding, and rubbed it.

"Oh, heavens." Why was she so weak around him? With each pass of those talented fingers, shivers of need danced over her skin, fracturing throughout her body into every nerve ending, reminding her of how he'd so easily learned how to command her body.

"You think to toss *this* away?" Over and over, he worked that tiny bundle of nerves, and when she couldn't hold back a moan, he grinned.

"For the good of your future," she managed to gasp out and curled the fingers of one hand into his thick, red hair. How was it that he had nearly sent her over that edge into bliss with hardly a touch?

His bark of laugh held an edge of bitterness she'd not heard from him before. "Haven't you guessed by now that I have no future without you?"

Tremors went through her chest to seize about her heart. "You can't throw it all away because of me."

"It's my damned decision. And don't you think love is worth more than that?" Then he gripped her inner thighs and splayed her open, encouraged one of her legs over his shoulder. "Damn, I'll never tire of eating you out, hearing you spend."

The words filled her with warmth. He wasn't a poet, but perhaps he didn't need to be, yet anticipation battled with anxiety in her belly. "It's for the best, and you know it." Diana kept her fingers buried in his hair, holding him to her but wanting to push him away. "We can't—" Her voice cut off in a squeak as he put his mouth to her button.

He chuckled and the vibrations sent her into another level of delight and wonder. And he began the next stage of his seduction—or rather his last attempt at a plea to win her.

"Merciful heavens." From the moment he employed his lips

and hot tongue to her most sensitive, private parts, Diana slowly lost the last vestiges of her sanity. Though he'd treated her to this delight before, right now, she couldn't catch her breath, for with each nibble, every nip, all the swipes and strokes of his tongue, she was hurled higher and higher into pleasure, into a world he alone had introduced her to.

He has made me fly in so many ways.

Wild sensation coursed through her body that she shook from it. Tears unashamedly fell to her cheeks, for everything was too big, too much, too overwhelming… too sad. Losing him fast on the heels of losing her father would certainly bury her. Never once did the viscount shy away from his work. He was a man bent on tossing her over the edge, and she hovered there, trapped, waiting with a hammering heart for him to give her up into that dark void.

Then she could finally think clearly again.

But he didn't. Not even when she begged him. Repeatedly, not caring her maid might hear if she was about. "Nathaniel, please, leave off!"

He merely grunted and kept her poised on the razor's edge, pinning her there again and again with every penetrating stroke of his tongue, each calculated nibble, every new torment of suction on that swollen nubbin until she squirmed and bucked against his face, praying for some sort of relief. She curled her hand into his hair alternately to shove him away and cease the exquisite torment but also to hold him to her tighter, guide him to exactly where she needed him.

How can I give him up, but how can I ruin his legacy to do that?

"Oh, oh, oh…" Her body shook; the relentless pressure in her lower belly built and coiled and stacked. Fearing she would break apart, Diana squirmed, but he gripped her hip tighter to keep her in place.

When he chuckled against her flesh, it was almost the end of her, but he kept on as if he were the rake he used to be.

"Nathaniel!" She shook as tears of pleasure rolled down her

cheeks. Her back arched of its own accord, which put her deeper into his care. "I am going to break."

"That is the purpose of this exercise." Then he followed the comment with a particularly strong bit of suction.

"I need—Ah!" The dam holding back the mounting pressure within broke. She shattered in spectacular fashion, fell into that black void full of the most wonderful bliss as her inner walls convulsed with a violent release. A half-muffled scream left her throat, for it was so glorious, and he would surely leave a hole in her life when they parted.

The viscount glanced up, but she was barely aware as she floated in a realm not bound to Earth. "Because I'm a bastard, come again for me, show me how much your body wants me. And remember, Diana, you are the *only* woman I ever want to share such intimacy with for the remainder of my life."

It was a sweet sentiment that marked large growth from him, and while her heart trembled, she remained resolute. Despite the fact her body shook, he continued to worry her swollen, hypersensitive button. When he inserted two fingers, pumping them in and out of her convulsing passage, she writhed against his hand while imagining those fingers were his length spearing into her. Then he twisted those digits as he'd done once before to massage a spot on her inner walls that separated her soul from her body.

"Oh, heavens!" The words were drawn out in a keening wail. Thinking was beyond her as Diana hurtled over the edge into a second hard release that stole her breath and rendered her temporarily unable to move. Her thighs trembled in time to her racing pulse, while flutters ran riot in her core as strong contractions rocked through her. Finally, when the viscount was finished, he withdrew his fingers and pulled away yet he gently guided her leg off his shoulder until she stood on unsure footing.

"I adore watching you come undone." There was no mistaking the smugness in his voice. "God, Diana, how can you not know how good we are together?"

She hadn't the strength to deny his words, but for the good of his future, she would remain firm in her decision. "Please leave. You are making things worse."

"Not until you give me the words I'm longing to hear." Stepping briefly away, he fumbled at his discarded clothing for a handkerchief which he used to wipe the moisture from his face. "If you prove stubborn, I'll match that because I know I'm right in this."

Seconds later, he caught her in his arms and then tossed her onto the bed, and she fell once more into heated sensations that prevented her from all common sense.

CHAPTER SIXTEEN

*S**HE IS SO** fucking beautiful, both inside and out, how can she possibly think we aren't exactly perfect for each other?*

As Diana lay sprawled in the middle of the bed, Nathaniel soon joined her, and seconds later, he claimed her lips in a searing kiss. Yes, he was angry and confused and perhaps feeling a bit vulnerable, but he wasn't going to step out of her life without trying once more to win her over and secure her promise.

"Shall I continue?" Her arms around his shoulders gave him hope, for if she hadn't wished for this coupling, she would have kicked his arse from the room without prejudice.

"Are you done pleading your case, then?" One of her light-brown eyebrows arched in challenge, for that's what she did best with him.

"Ha!" How much did he adore her? "I won't be the one pleading by the time we are finished this night."

"So arrogant of you to assume that."

With need pulsing through his impossibly hard shaft, Nathaniel lost no time in exploring her body with his palms and fingertips. Damn, her curves would drive him mad before long, but he looked forward to the descent. Never could he have enough of her form, and one of these days, he would have time to explore every inch of her, but tonight was for a different outcome entirely. When he brushed her pebbled nipples with his knuckles, bent his head to take one of them into his mouth, her shuddering breath and moan made him chuckle.

"I adore how responsive you are." Every touch, every caress he gave her provoked a sound or a shiver. After what had occurred in William's drawing room, he didn't think he would be given the chance to have her in his bed again let alone another opportunity to try and win her heart, and he refused to waste a second of it.

In many ways, he'd been preparing for this very moment the whole of his adult life.

"I'll show you responsive, Holdcraft." Slowly, and holding his gaze the whole time, Diana edged a hand down his torso, slid it along his abdomen, and then finally, she cupped his equipage with a firm hand. He uttered a chuckle mixed with a groan.

"You wouldn't." The bewitching twinkle in her eyes meant wicked things ahead for him, and he couldn't wait. It also meant she was coming 'round to his way of thinking.

"I would indeed. Why should you have all the power?" With a giggle, she moved her hand. Gently at first then with more friction and authority, she stroked her curled fingers up and down his length. "Did you mean what you said?"

What the devil? He couldn't think while she fondled him. "I said many things."

"Earlier tonight, that I'm the only woman you want in your bed from now on... or something to that effect."

The darling woman suffered from insecurities the same as him, yet she wished to run from them instead of talk about them. "I did. There is no one else for me except you, from now to eternity."

That shocked him as much as it apparently did her.

"Oh." Her hand never left his member, and her touch, the floral scent of her, the warmth of her body against his all worked at his undoing.

"Diana..." His shaft tightened, thickened from her handling, but she ignored his warning and continued her ministrations.

Over and over, her palm and fingers glided up and down his prick. She brushed the pads of her fingers along the sensitive tip, and as he sucked in a breath, she pressed her lips to his shoulder, nipped the skin with her teeth while guiding her touch down to fondle his stones, squeeze them, presumably in a bid to make certain he never forgot her. Nathaniel jerked in her hold; he wouldn't last at this point. Needing an outlet, a distraction so that he wouldn't spend prematurely, he brought his mouth crashing down on hers.

For one second, her fingers paused as she kissed him back, but as he fenced with her tongue, perhaps implored her to accept his suit, she resumed her attentions on his shaft. Up and down. Twist. Up and down. Twist. Faster and faster with varying degrees of tension and friction.

The woman is going to kill me.

And he looked forward to a lifetime of it, because he *would* win her. "Hold, else I'll come on you instead of in you." He stilled her hand, but damn he couldn't wait to claim her body, for as many times as she'd let him tonight.

"Nothing is stopping you." Holding his gaze the whole time, she moved her hands to his chest and kissed him, lightly nipped his bottom lip. "Reassure me, Nathaniel. Show me that if I choose it, a future with you won't prove a disaster, that my selfish choice won't be your downfall."

The poor thing. Love for her built even stronger because she only thought of him and what she assumed he needed and wanted from his own life.

"I'll do my level best." This might be the most important bedding he'd ever participated it. Pushing her arms above her head, he threaded their fingers together while settling comforta-bly between her raised knees. "Everything I said tonight has been nothing but truth." Then, peering into her eyes, he penetrated her warm and welcoming body, went as deep as he could into her body, so she'd have no doubts about how much he wanted her in all the ways that mattered.

"Oh, goodness." Her back arched, which sent him ever deeper. As her eyes closed, tears slipped to her cheeks. "It's too much, all of it is."

Not knowing if she referred to the coupling or recent events, he squeezed her fingers then moved within her. When he would have gone frantic and hard for this joining, he changed his mind at the last second, for perhaps she needed slow and gentle tonight; she needed reassurance, and he would always give her that.

"Nathaniel, I…" She clutched at his hands, but her words dissolved into a sigh of pleasure.

For several moments, he stroked into her more tenderly than he'd ever done in recent years. Diana had made all the difference in his life, and he wished to show her that. In the midst of his lovemaking, he released her hands in order to hold her head between his palms. Slowly, he kissed her as if he had all the time in the world while ignoring his own needs. With a moan of approval, Diana clung to him, wrapped her arms around his shoulders and her legs about his as she moved her body in time to his.

When more tears fell to her cheeks, he kissed them away as he loved her with every ounce of feeling he could muster.

Then urgency reminded him that he couldn't last and he wasn't a young man any longer. Quickly, he changed his rhythm. Without hesitation, she matched him, met each stroke because that had been her wont all along.

"I'm so close," she whispered as her head thrashed on the pillow.

"As am I."

When she put a hand between them to bedevil her own button, he almost lost his hold on control. Wanting to be the one to send her over, he batted her hand away only to rub that nubbin with varying degrees of friction that he knew she liked.

"Why must you torture me so?" she asked around panting breaths, as she dug her fingernails into his shoulders, his back, even his buttocks.

Those tiny pinpricks of pain spurred him onward and sent him hurtling toward the edge. "That's part of the fun." He worked doubly hard at sending her over the brink, and the brief reprieve from thrusting was most welcome. Quicker he moved his fingertips on that nubbin. Harder, then with soothing strokes, he worked that tiny bundle of nerves.

"Nathaniel!" Diana's body stiffened. Her back arched; her toes pointed. She grabbed a fistful of the coverlet as she shattered in his hold. "Oh, oh, *oh!*"

The expression of bliss on her face almost had him following her down into that void, but he clenched his jaw and staved off the inevitable. As a flush of arousal covered her chest, he encouraged one of her legs upward while she wrapped the other about his waist. "Let's see how quickly you can go over again, hmm?"

He withdrew from her passage merely to savor the moment of spearing into her tight, welcoming passage again. Damn, but that was one of his most favorite parts, and doing this with Diana would easily become an addiction, one he never wanted to find his way out of.

Then he was lost to the wonder of her body, of joining with her, rising up the hill with her, falling down the other side, and repeating the trip until they both panted and surged against each other. Faster his hips worked. Deeper he stroked in the attempt to touch her soul. Over and over, they indulged in a dance as old as time itself.

I would do anything for you. Just take that chance with me.

Diana came apart in his arms the same time release rushed through him to heat every nerve ending and point throughout his body. He called out her name while a keening cry left her throat, and the contractions in her core threatened to suck him under once more. As his shaft pulsed, he ground his hips into hers, fucked her until the very end in a futile effort to prolong the joining, but of course, he was spent.

They rode the waves of bliss as one. As the chaos and pleasure calmed, with a sigh, he collapsed on top of her then rolled to his side and pulled her with him. "Ah, damn, how can you not see how utterly fantastic we are together?"

"I…" She buried her face into the crook of his shoulder. Moisture dampened his skin as he realized she was crying again.

"Did I do something wrong?"

"No." She uttered a sigh mixed with a giggle, and the sound went straight to his heart. "I think it's me who is wrong." When she lifted her head, met his gaze, there was such love in those sapphire depths that he caught his breath. "But I won't change my mind." Another wave of tears welled in her eyes.

"Dearest, you wouldn't be so upset if you didn't think your choice wasn't the one you truly wish to make." At least he hoped so.

Diana shook her head. The sadness in her expression nearly broke his heart all over again. "I've told you my reasoning. It's better that I let you move on and find someone else who can give you what you need."

"Why must she prove so stubborn?" Nathaniel pulled her closer to his side, found and held her gaze with his. "You'd sacrifice a future with me for that?"

"Yes, of course."

"Why?"

When she shrugged, her skin brushed over his and left heated tendrils of awareness behind. "Because I love you and want you to have everything you desire." She pressed her lips together as they trembled. "If that isn't with me, so be it."

How had he never considered courting a strong-willed woman like her before? Perhaps because he'd wanted her all along, but, damn, he adored her. "Did you ever think that perhaps it's society who says I need those things? Did you ever think to ask me what *I* want for my *own* life?"

"No, I just assumed…" Diana frowned as she considered him. "What are you saying?"

"The same thing I said in the drawing room." He brought her closer still and brushed his lips over hers. "Darling, I desire *you*, I want *you*, I need *you* because I love *you*. Not for what you can possibly give me, even if fate was kind and a miracle was at play. I don't require any of those things to live a happy life, but I *do* need you."

Skepticism lay stamped on her face as her light-brown hair tumbled from its pins and the silver strands glimmered in the dim illumination from the single candle on the bureau. "I don't know… Everything is so important, though."

"As are you." He held her gaze, almost willed her to understand, to see it from his point of view. "It matters not to me if I never have an heir. Let the solicitors figure that out after I'm off this mortal coil. Perhaps they can find a direct male descendant of my father's."

"But—"

A tiny huff escaped him. "A title is a title, but it can't hold a candle to love, to finding the person you want to spend the remainder of life with, to being content with who you are." And that was finally what he was. Diana had helped him to see that.

Slowly, she shook her head. "What if you want children for yourself?"

"Then we can adopt one of the multitudes of orphans in London, and in the end, I'll still have you."

For long moments, she frowned at him, regarded him with a slightly tilted head. "I'm not worth tossing away your legacy, though."

"Like hell you're not. And besides, they are two different things entirely." When she didn't appear convinced, he knew it was time to play the one card left to him. "I shall return in a twinkling."

"Where are you going?" she asked as he rolled off the bed to rummage in his discarded clothing.

"One moment." After pulling a much-folded piece of paper from the pocket of his waistcoat, Nathaniel returned to the bed, where he gently unfolded it, catching a ring into his hand and hiding it in his palm before she spied it. "I have taken your advice."

"Oh?"

He nodded. "I've written my own bit of poetry. For you. And if that doesn't convince you of my feelings and intent then nothing will."

"You wrote poetry?" Her eyes rounded with surprise. "For me?"

"I did." Feeling a bit cheeky, he winked. "Shall I read it, or are you determined to stick by your original decision?"

"Don't be an arse, Holdcraft."

Which meant yes.

"Bear in mind, this isn't nearly as lovely as Keats can do, but as it's my first attempt, I'm allowed a bit of latitude." Then he cleared his throat, consulted the paper even though he knew the words off by heart, and he started to speak. "I call it *An Ode to My Future Wife*."

Her gaze was glued to his face.

"In her eyes, there are a billion stars where I dream, but in her lips, I lose myself in the myriad of possibilities for they are so sweet.

"Named after a goddess, she is that to me; in her kisses I am reborn, for she is as fierce as a huntress but as magical as a deity.

"In her touch, my world shivers into sharper focus, she has reconstructed my future merely with her words.

"There is beauty in how she moves, but it is the hope she gives in the music of her laughter that brings me to my knees.

"What have I done to deserve such a woman? I will do whatever she desires so that I might keep her, for there is no one else in this world I love and adore as much as she.

"My Diana, my lover, my world… my heart."

She bounced her gaze from the paper to his face. "Oh, Nathaniel." Tears welled again in her eyes, magnifying the blue. "That was lovely." There was a decided tremble in her chin.

"Never say you have no talent. Truly, you should continue to pen poetry."

"You were my inspiration, of course." Then he opened his palm, took the ring and held the shank with his thumb and forefinger. "This is part of a parure from my estate. It once belonged to one of my aunts, who died shortly after she married, but in my heart I know the whole part and parcel belongs to you."

"Why?"

"The middle stone is because I adore seeing you in lavender, and the sapphires remind me of your eyes." A central round amethyst winked in the low light, surrounded by tiny round sapphires and diamonds that winked like mad every time he moved the trinket. "Marry me, Diana. I love you, *have* loved you, will *always* love you, to the end of my natural life and perhaps beyond."

A tear slipped down her cheek. "You don't play fair."

"Of course I don't, not when love is in the offing." When she remained quiet, he tried one last time. "If you feel you might be bored with me, then let us collaborate together and do something that will help people in London. Something that will be a legacy for us. We'll create our own charity or cause, hell, we can open our own bookshop, I don't care. I merely want you by my side because you make me better, make me want to strive to be the man you think I am."

What else could he say to convince her that he was genuine?

Diana struggled into a sitting position with her glorious body on display. "You are making the changes, have started that right after meeting me, so there is no need to think you aren't a good man already."

At least she'd noticed. "And?" He didn't want to rush her, but damn, he'd been hovering on the edge of hope for a bit, and he required an answer.

Tears fell to her cheeks. She glanced from the ring he held to his face. Finally, she nodded. "How can I deny you anything?

How can I deny myself even if I wonder if you'll regret this some years down the line?"

"I won't. I promise."

She nodded. "No, you might not, but for what it's worth, I do love you to distraction."

"Ha!" Relief twisted down his spine, but victory swelled his chest. "Does that mean you'll marry me?" He needed to hear the words.

"Yes," she said in a choked whisper and followed it with a nod. "I'll marry you and be happy to do so."

Excitement plowed into him, yet he resisted the urge to shout his happiness from the window. "What of William's objections?"

"They don't matter." Her shrug only lifted on shoulder. "He has his own life to live. This one is mine."

"Ah, sweeting, I am beside myself with joy." Taking her left hand, when he slipped the ring onto her fourth finger, his own hand shook. "By the by, I *did* ask Percy's permission, which he granted."

"How sweet of you." Leaning over, she brushed her lips over his. Another wave of awareness shivered through him. When she met his gaze, a wealth of emotions shone in her eyes, the strongest of which was love. "My heart is so full it frightens me. What if this marriage is as cold and uncaring as my first?"

"I can promise you that will not happen. I am not Atterbury, and I'm far too madly in love with you to ever ignore you. I might as well cut off my hands." When she would have protested, he hauled her into his arms so that she straddled his lap. Then he kissed her, and continued to do so until she was equally convinced of his fervor. "Let me recover for an hour or so and then I'll show you the depths of my regard."

"Oh, Nathaniel." Diana snuggled into his chest. The warmth of her breath on his skin worked to arouse him all over again. "I already know. You've never hidden it."

"Perhaps I didn't, for in you, I saw my future from the first."

To be honest, he was tired of hiding his heart in shallow

liaisons and never truly connecting with a woman. All of that was over, and he couldn't wait to see where his life led next. Wherever it was, with her by his side, he was certain it would prove spectacular.

EPILOGUE

November 14, 1817
No. 10
Bedford Square
Mayfair, London

NATHANIEL STOOD AT one of the drawing room windows with a slight grin curving his lips. Dried brown leaves danced and swirled on the pavement, pushed along in a dance by an autumnal breeze. From where he stood, the ambient chill in the air seeped through the glass, but that didn't bother him, for it just meant an extra excuse to snuggle with his wife.

Earlier this afternoon, he'd married the love of his life, Diana. Yes, he'd waited five months to finally make her officially his, but then, she'd been observing mourning for her father, and though she still had one more month left in that period, she'd decided that since she was already a widow and because the ceremony was held at home in private with a very limited guest list, that society matrons would understand.

Not that it mattered, since she didn't need their blessing any longer. She'd chosen him and didn't need to relaunch herself into society to land him.

When he'd said vows to her today, he'd meant every word. No longer was he the same man he'd been before he'd met her. From the first day she'd come back into his life, he'd not looked at another woman let alone tried to flirt with one. That's how much

Diana had changed what he wanted from his existence.

"Nathaniel? What are you doing in here?" The sound of his wife's voice sent a shiver down his spine, for she always managed to affect him. "William and Mama have finally left. I never thought they'd get on with their day."

"They lingered quite a while." When she joined him, he immediately slipped his arms about her. "God, you're gorgeous today."

"Because I'm glowing or due to my gown?"

"Both?" However, the gown she'd chosen to wear for their nuptial ceremony *was* exceptional. Made from dove-gray taffeta, ruched black satin ribbon lined the low bodice, the wrists of the long sleeves, and the hem of the skirt. A row of small jet buttons decorated the back. "I like the simple lines of the frock, but I'll adore it even more seeing it on the floor of our bedroom."

"Ha. There is time enough for that, and I do have plans for you in that regard." A smile curved her lips. As always, his world brightened. "William is just annoyed that Mama has turned her attentions and is trying to find a match for him."

"It might be good for him. Marrying certainly was for me."

"So charming." She laid a palm against the side of face. "Do you feel any different as a married man?"

"Not really. The only difference is I can finally spend every day and night with you instead of a handful of hours here and there." Which he couldn't wait to begin. "Oh, there is some news I forgot to share with you since the ceremony took all of my attention."

"What? Is it good news? Lord knows we've had enough of bad for a while."

"That we have."

Over the past five months, planning a small, discreet wedding had been met with a few problems gleaned from last year when horrible, unexpected weather had destroyed food supplies and disrupted shipping of products, such as stationery, or even procuring the most mundane things like ribbon and fabric and buttons. To say nothing of food scarcity at times, due to everyone in England trying to obtain the same things to eat.

But they got through it with cursing and tears.

Also, discussions to renovate his townhouse and redo it into Diana's style had been thwarted by much the same issues. Eventually, they'd be able to take care of all the ideas they had between them, but right now, they were revising their original plans.

Not that he minded, for all he'd wanted from the engagement was her.

"Well?" she asked with anticipation in her expression as he tugged a folded piece of paper from the interior pocket of his tailcoat and then gave it to her.

"We have secured the lease on the shop off Oxford Street," he said with a grin as she read the confirmation letter with shaking hands.

"How wonderful!" Joy reflected in her eyes as she looked at him. "Now we can move ahead with the plans for the bookshop and start stocking it."

"Indeed. If all goes well, we can open after the first of the year." Caught up in the excitement of something they'd both wanted since becoming engaged, he pulled her into his arms. "You will be the most attractive shop owner."

"Do stop, Holdcraft." But she gave him that special smile she reserved only for him. "I am looking forward to everything about this new venture of ours, but especially the nights we will set aside for you to read poetry aloud for intimate gatherings. Including your own."

"We shall see." Ever since he'd written his first poem for her, she'd encouraged him to continue on and see where his muse led him. "I don't know that I'm confident enough to share my work with the public."

"You will be." With her arms about his middle, Diana laid her head on his shoulder. "I can't believe we're married and soon-to-be shop owners."

"Are you pleased with that?" Surely, she wasn't entertaining regrets already.

"I am, and I can't wait to see what else we'll get up to together."

"Mmm." Feeling far too amorous to linger in the drawing room longer, Nathaniel swept her up into his arms. "Perhaps we should make inroads into finding that out right now by consummating this union."

Her squeal made him grin and went straight to his stones. "Obviously, we've come together many times over the past five months, but since I adore how you set my body on fire, I'll most definitely agree."

"This afternoon's session will be long and quite thorough. We must work up an appetite to do justice to my cook's wedding dinner, you see." A hunger of a different sort chased through his insides, for he couldn't believe the woman in his arms was finally his and they could start their life together.

"Such bragging, Nathaniel." She tsked her tongue. "It's almost as if you're trying to make up for shoddy attention between the sheets."

"You should know that's quite the bammer, but I suppose I'll need to refresh your memory," he said as he carried her out of the room toward the stairs. "Planning for this day and your trousseau has apparently rotted your memory."

She giggled then pressed her lips to the side of his neck. "I look forward to your primer then."

Never had he made his way up to his suite so quickly. Once he had her behind the closed door, he set her onto her feet then trapped her between the wooden panel and his chest, kissing her at his leisure, for they had all the time in the world.

It was mindboggling how a man's whole outlook and direction changed when he decided to chase something entirely different. That was also when he stumbled upon the most wonderful gift he never knew he wanted. And now, he couldn't imagine how he'd made it this far in life without her.

Something to think about, indeed.

The End

About the Author

Sandra Sookoo is an award winning and *USA Today* bestselling author of over 200 books who firmly believes every person deserves acceptance and a happy ending. That is why her characters are not in the usual style and oftentimes struggle with things out of the norm. She's written for publication since 2008. Most days you can find her creating scandal and mischief in the Regency-era, serendipity and happenstance in the Victorian era, or historical romantic suspense complete with mystery and intrigue. Reading is a lot like eating chocolates—you can't just have one book. Give her the chance with one book and you'll be hooked.

When she's not wearing out computer keyboards or mice, Sandra spends time with her real-life Prince Charming in Central Indiana where she also runs a gourmet cookie business and makes moments count with the man because the key to life is laughter. Inspired to storytelling by Walt Disney since the age of ten, when her soul gets bogged down and her imagination flags, a trip to Walt Disney World is in order. Nothing fills the well and fuels her dreams more than the land of eternal happy endings, hope and love stories.

Also of note, Sandra DOES NOT use AI in any of her writing.

Stay in Touch

Sign up for Sandra's bi-monthly newsletter and you'll be given exclusive excerpts, cover reveals before the general public as well as opportunities to enter contests you won't find anywhere else.

Just send an email to sandrasookoo@yahoo.com with SUB-SCRIBE in the subject line.

Or follow/friend her on social media:
Facebook: facebook.com/sandra.sookoo
Facebook Author Page: facebook.com/sandrasookooauthor
Pinterest: pinterest.com/sandrasookoo
Instagram: instagram.com/sandrasookoo
BookBub Page: bookbub.com/authors/sandra-sookoo